Barren Womb

Denise M. Walker

This is a work of fiction. Names. Characters, and incidents are the product of the author's imagination or are used fictitiously. Any resemblance to actual persons, living or dead, events, or locales is entirely coincidental.

Armor of Hope Writing & Publishing Services, LLC
www.armorofhopewritingservices.com

Scripture quotations taken from the New American Standard Bible® (NASB), Copyright © 1960, 1962, 1963, 1968, 1971, 1972, 1973, 1975, 1977, 1995 by The Lockman Foundation, Used by permission. www.Lockman.org

Scripture quotations marked (NLT) are taken from the Holy Bible, New Living Translation, copyright ©1996, 2004, 2015 by Tyndale House Foundation. Used by permission of Tyndale House Publishers, a Division of Tyndale House Ministries, Carol Stream, Illinois 60188. All rights reserved.

Printed in the United States

First Printing, 2020

Editor: Chandra Sparks Splond

Cover Design: Denise M. Walker

ISBN: 978-1-7336134-4-6

Dedication

I want to begin dedicating this book to my nephew, Rayshawd Dixon. While Barren Womb was in its final stages, you left us unexpectantly. Your Uncle Brian, BJ, and I will never forget you. We love and miss you dearly. You were a true blessing to your mom and the rest of us.

In addition, to the two mighty women of God, who led me to Christ and are gone on to be with the Lord, Rose Johnson and Christine Reeves. You will always be in my heart. I am eternally grateful for the seeds you sowed into my life while here on Earth.

Finally, I want to dedicate this book to all barren women. Know that God can do anything but fail. Also, know that barrenness is beyond the physical; it's also spiritual. Christ is the answer.

Barren

not productive, lacking, devoid, unfruitful, infertile, desolate, depleted, ineffective, yielding no return because of inactivity, or idle

"O God, you are my God; I earnestly search for you.
My soul thirsts for you; my whole body longs for you
in this parched and weary land where there is no water."
(Psalm 63:1 NLT)

ACKNOWLEDGMENTS

Thank you, Lord Jesus, for bringing me out of my barren places with your love. Thank you for healing, delivering and making me whole again. All that I thought I needed is found in you. Thank you for using me as a vessel to pour out my heart through this novel. May the women who read it be set free by your remarkable power.

To my husband, Brian Walker, thank you once again for your love and for always supporting me. I love you with all my heart.

To my son, BJ, thank you. You are an incredible young man. Always put God first. I love you, son.

TABLE OF CONTENTS

PROLOGUE

ears streaming, but feeling renewed, Hannah Jefferson was up next. She stood and moved slowly from the back of the room to share with the women of Giver of Life Ministries. Her friend, Robin, had invited her, promising that she would feel the love from the other women who had also experienced struggles and disappointments. Hannah wished there was another road she could have taken, but it wasn't her choice. Her walk to the front of the room felt like an eternity as she wiped away more tears and considered changing her mind and allowing the next woman to share.

He alone is my refuge, my place of safety... Hannah was comforted again by Psalm 91:2. God had given it to her in the sanctuary earlier. She sat and read it over and over. Hannah felt that God was reminding her that she was safe with him. As others prayed with her and led her to Christ, she let down her guard and chose to allow him in. She had never felt such peace in her life than just a few minutes ago, when she opened her heart to Christ. Hannah paused, wiped her eyes with a tissue and looked across the room before she began.

"I really don't know what to say. I've never been comfortable speaking in front of people I don't know," Hannah spoke into the microphone. She felt the unconditional love of Ms. Priscilla and Robin, who both nodded and smiled, giving her the courage to push forward.

"It's okay. You've got this, sis," Robin encouraged her from the front row.

"Well, I guess I'll share a little bit about myself. I am a wife and an educator. I feel I have walked through so much, yet I've been surrounded by so much love. The love just didn't seem like it was enough. I thought I could get over all that I'd been through in time. Then, not long ago, I was going to be a mother until..." Hannah stammered.

"Take your time," a dark-skinned woman with spiral curls stated from the back. Hannah looked around the room. Her heart raced. Her eyes landed on Ms. Priscilla again as she attempted to encourage her from her seat on the second row. She felt more comfortable as she smiled at one of the women who had loved her through all of her pain. She wasn't sure if the other women would embrace her.

We are our sister's keeper. The words rang in her ears as she continued to try to find the right words to speak. The women had recited them just before the fellowship began. Hannah still wasn't sure if she felt comfortable baring her soul in a roomful of strangers.

"Hannah, are you good?" Robin whispered.

"Yes. Well, as I was saying, I was going to be a mother until I found out it wasn't possible. As a result of that news, I've struggled. In addition, I continue to be rejected by the one person I've needed the most. I've said things to hurt others and cried a river of tears until I felt numb. I don't know if any of you can relate, but I finally decided to surrender my heart to God after really hearing Ms. Priscilla's words for the first time. I thought I could heal my own brokenness, but I realized I couldn't—no one could. Only God. I've learned so much, things I never understood, even as an adult. For one, I've come to understand that disappointment and rejection can lead you to the foot of the cross. Oftentimes, we think we know what we want, but if God is not a part of that equation, we'll find ourselves empty."

"Testify," an older woman on the front row shouted. Hannah smiled as the other women began to follow suit. Her heart melted as they allowed her to finish sharing her journey to true love.

CHAPTER ONE

One Year Earlier

Following the second full week with her new third graders at Rock Lake Elementary, Hannah Jefferson was ecstatic to see Friday afternoon. She returned to her classroom after a short department meeting, which was called once the students were released. She and the other third grade teachers had discussed specific standards to cover before the state assessment, which was months away. They talked about the third-grade field trip and reviewed more procedures and expectations for the year. Hannah's head swam with all the information. She had hundreds of notes in her planner. Her principal would constantly remind them that he expected them to remain one of the top elementary schools in Forest Park. Hannah appreciated the way Mr. Hall kept them ahead of the game and well trained, wanting to ultimately be the best school in Georgia, but it was exhausting at times.

Dang, the first month is always crazy.

As she attempted to organize her classroom, Hannah's cell phone began to vibrate. She walked over to her desk to see who was calling. It was Brittany. She smiled and hit the talk button.

"Hey, sis. How are you feeling today?" Brittany sang.

"Hey, baby sis. I'm feeling good. Just a little tired. How are you?" Hannah stated. She sat at her desk and pulled up her lesson plan template to drop that day's lesson into Monday's slot. She had gotten behind this week because they were still reviewing basic skills from the previous year. Next week, Hannah planned to begin the new curriculum.

"Well, you just wait until my niece or nephew starts growing. You're really going to need a pillow at work."

"Girl, you are so crazy." Hannah said, rubbing her belly, attempting to focus on her sister and her lesson plans at the same time. She and her husband,

Levi, were expecting their first child. She smiled at the thought of her twofold blessing. She was now rid of those horrible menstrual cycles for at least six months. Their blessing was conceived as she waited for her birth control refill. Hannah had been taking them since she was a teen, after the doctor told her dad about the large cysts that came and went from month to month. The doctor had adjusted the birth control pills after her appointment about a year ago due to her continued complaints about her painful cycles. Now, she was free, at least for a little while longer.

Hannah lay her phone down and pressed the speaker button, "How are your new courses going?" Hannah asked, remembering how much Brittany had complained about her course load last semester, but she had pushed through it. Hannah was proud of her baby sister. She would soon become a nurse, something she had shared with Hannah more than once.

"They're okay so far. I have three exams to study for. This nursing program ain't no joke."

"I bet, but you can do it. You got this. How are things going with you and Travis?" Hannah asked, flipping through her reading textbook for the title of the story she wanted to focus on for the remainder of next week.

"We're good. He's stressing with his graduation requirements. He had to pick up an extra class that he didn't know about."

"I bet that's a lot."

"Yeah. He's determined to graduate on time. He already has an internship and possible job offer at this accounting firm in Atlanta. He decided he wants to open his own office someday."

"That's awesome, Brit."

"I know. I wish I was getting ready to be done so I can start my nursing career."

"It will come real soon. Stay focused on your goals.

"And how is your friend, Kelsey?"

"She's doing good, working most of the time and trying to maintain her course load. I told her it was going to be hard trying to get an apartment off campus."

"Are her parents able to help any?"

"A little. She asked me to be her roommate, but you know my part-time job at Marshall's isn't paying a lot. I would have to get a second job."

"Yeah. That sounds like a lot, Brit. I guess try to stay on campus as long as you can and save some money."

"I plan to. You know Mama don't have anything extra, and there's no need for me to call my daddy. He hasn't done much at all for me and Malik."

"I hear you. I know that's not easy for you and my baby brother."

"It's not. Like I told you before, he hardly even calls."

"Right, I hate that."

"Anyway, I'm so glad I decided on Clayton State. I didn't like it when I first got here, but I made it through my first two years, and the professors have been awesome. Plus, you know I always enjoy hanging out with you and your family," Brittany stated.

"You know I was excited when you first told me you chose my alma mater. I knew you would enjoy it."

"Yeah. Mama still gets mad when I don't come to Roswell as much, but I just want her to stop drinking. That's why Malik and I worked so hard to get out of there. I was determined. I'm working my butt off to being able to take care of myself."

"I understand. I hate that you and Malik felt you had to get away from Mama."

"I mean, you know I love Mama, but she's so angry all the time. I don't know if she ever got over Grandma's death. She talks about her a lot, and you know Granddad has never really come around either. She's tried reaching out to him a few times over the years, but he doesn't do the same for her, and she doesn't really talk to anyone else but Aunt Loretta. Not to mention, she seems to still be angry with Daddy because he left when Malik and I were toddlers."

"I remember you telling me that. I can hardly remember you and Malik's dad being there. I was so young. I only remember those boyfriends. They were horrible."

"Yeah, she just let those dudes mistreat her for so many years."

"Right, and I still wonder why she seems to hate Daddy and I so much too."

"Facts. I don't know what went on between her and Mr. Monroe," said Brittany.

"I really think our family has to talk more about our problems."

"Well, that ain't gon' happen with Mama. She holds so much inside, and when she starts drinking, she is a whole other person."

"I know," Hannah replied, her thoughts drifting.

She thought back to her childhood, if that's what she would call it. The pain of her mom's verbal and physical abuse, being taken from her, and going to live with Aunt Loretta would forever be etched in her memory. She couldn't understand why her mom wouldn't stop drinking so she could return home, but her mom didn't seem to be concerned about Hannah, only about the men in her life. The molestation started soon after moving in with Aunt Loretta. Back then, Hannah would've chosen being adopted over her spirit being shattered and the rejection she'd endured. Today, she was grateful for her dad. He had rescued her. Hannah didn't have many immediate family members. Both of her dad's parents had passed away, as well as his aunt who raised him and Uncle Joseph. Hannah had considered checking out that ancestry.com site to learn more about her family, but she would dismiss it each time it popped up on her computer. Her mom and dad had shared a few details over the years. Hannah remembered some things about her mom's mom, Grandma Liz. It was so long ago. However, she did cherish that Grandma Liz was allowed to name her. She remembered being taught the meaning of her name. It was biblical, and it meant *grace and favored*. At the moment, Hannah felt she needed more grace from her mom. She was thankful for the family in her life but hoped that things would get better between her and her mom someday soon, at least for the sake of her child knowing his or her other family.

"Sis, are you listening?"

"Yeah, I hear you," Hannah replied.

"Are you okay?" Brittany asked.

"Yeah. I'm fine."

"I was telling you I tried calling to check on her the other day, and Mama started talking about you and your dad's family again, so I told her I had to go."

"I guess things won't change any time soon," Hannah said with sadness.

"I don't know, but I'm so tired of hearing her talking about you like you aren't her daughter."

"Well, I hope she comes around someday soon. I've been thinking about her a lot lately. Been thinking about reaching out to her again," Hannah replied, holding back the tears that would soon come. She felt much like the woman who was forced to wear an A on her clothing in Scarlet Letter, the book they had read back in high school. Her teacher was an older woman and loved to read classics. Hannah only remembered how the woman in the book was rejected. She could relate all too well. She too had been shunned by the one individual who should have embraced and protected her from the world's wrath.

"I don't know, sis. You don't ever know when Mama is going to start tripping."

"I know, but I feel like it's time. It's been two years since we've even talked, and even then, she was so distant."

"Yeah, but her and Auntie Loretta need to be ashamed, not coming to you and Levi's wedding. They've treated you bad for so long. Blaming you for what Uncle Malcolm did to you. Dirty dog."

"I know. When they didn't show up, that really hurt me, but I do want my baby to have the opportunity to know Mama."

"I feel you. I just don't know. I mean, Mama seemed to care more about Malik than anything. He told me that Mama got so upset when he decided to go into the Marines. She didn't seem to care one way or another about me living on campus an hour away from home. She didn't have a talk with me before I left as she did with Malik. She only said, 'Don't come back here with no babies once you start over at that college.' I couldn't believe her. She never says stuff like that to Malik."

"Yeah, that's not cool. We shouldn't feel like a disappointment to her. But just try to focus on your classes. Hopefully we can get together one of these weekends and try to get Mama to have lunch with us. Maybe we can have a heart to heart with her."

"I hear you, sis, but don't get your hopes up that she'll agree."

"I really hope we can. Well, I'm glad you called."

"Me too. You know I tell you all the time how lucky you are to have Mr. Monroe in your life. Between Mama and my trifling daddy, I don't know what to do sometime. I told you Malik don't want to have anything to do with Daddy. I still try to stay in touch with him, but he's a hot mess too."

"Well, sis, you know I'm here if you need me. I do thank God for Daddy and Aunt Melissa and Uncle Joseph. They've been great."

"I wish I could say the same about my dad's side of the family," Brittany said before saying goodbye.

Hannah ended the call and placed her phone on her desk. Covering her face with her hands, she reflected on her sister's words as tears welled in her eyes. *When will Mama come around? All I've ever wanted is a relationship with her. Why does she seem to hate me?* Hannah thought, crying. At only twenty-five years old, Hannah felt she was too young to have experienced so much. Now, she just wanted to have a healthy child and be a good mother, something she had yet to experience.

Although her siblings had not been uprooted from their mom as she had, she was worried about them. At twenty and eighteen, Brittany and Malik had to fight through a lot to both graduate high school with honors. Malik had chosen against college for now, but still enlisted in the Marines, and Brittany's dream was to become a registered nurse someday. Maybe she was the lucky one, she guessed, going to live with her dad at twelve, but she admired her brother and sister's perseverance without much help from either parent. They had all pressed through regardless of their circumstances.

Struggling to overcome her past, Hannah's dad did everything he could to help her through it all. She eventually graduated with a degree in education, fulfilling her dream of empowering youth after taking so long to make up her mind. She wanted them to know they were loved and accepted, so she considered becoming a social worker or a counselor. Then, she realized she wanted to help shape their minds and assist in growing their knowledge. Her decision was made after visiting several career fairs and being invited to observe an elementary school teacher who attended school with her dad. After several weeks of observing and helping out, Hannah fell in love with the third-grade students and the curriculum.

Despite her pain and disappointments, Hannah was glad things were moving in a more positive direction after so many years of being disconnected from Brittany and Malik. She would continue to wait patiently for her mom to come around.

What hurt did Mama experience to cause her to be so angry and drink her life away? Hannah sighed.

Finally, Hannah dried her eyes with a tissue from the apple-shaped container on her desk. She stood, walked over and sat in her cushioned chair at the guided reading table by the door, rubbing her belly again. *Yes, things are looking up. We'll be a family soon. That's what I should be focused on right now.* Hannah thought, more tears forming. She lay her head back, closed her eyes, and continued to gently rub her belly over and over, smiling. This was a dream come true for her and Levi, and she couldn't be happier.

"I promise to do my best for you, even though Mama was never really there for me," she said, looking down at her belly. Hannah remained at the table for a few more minutes, taking in the silence.

She then stood and walked back over to her desk, preparing to head home. As she lifted her cell phone to toss it into her purse, a calendar alert flashed a reminder on the screen.

"Dang. I forgot about my hair appointment with Ms. Priscilla tomorrow." Hannah always looked forward to their talks. Ms. Priscilla had been sliding the gospel message of Christ into their conversations since Hannah had located her shop after her previous hairdresser moved away. She had to give it to her, Ms. Priscilla was definitely persistent.

After checking her phone, Hannah tossed it in her purse, grabbed her school bag and headed out to her car. As she was walking down the third-grade hall, she ran into her friend, Robin. They had attended Clayton State University together and now both taught at Rock Lake in the same grade, just up the hall from each other. Hannah hoped her eyes weren't red. She didn't feel like talking about why she had been crying.

"Hey. What are you doing tomorrow?" Robin asked.

"I have a hair appointment in the morning but nothing in the afternoon. Levi has to work, so he'll be exhausted and only want to rest all day once he gets in," Hannah explained.

"I bet he will. You don't look like you need a hair appointment. Your twist outs always look beautiful. I'll be glad when I can get my little twigs to do that."

"Girl, thank you. Your hair is beautiful too. I just need Ms. P to do a trim and press. I know it won't last long."

"You might be there a few hours."

"I know. Don't remind me," Hannah replied with a sigh.

"Alright. Well, tell Minister Priscilla hello for me."

"I will. You know I could talk to her all day long. She encourages me every time I sit in her chair."

"Yes, ma'am. She ain't no joke. We're both still waiting for you to come back and visit us at church. It's been weeks since we've seen you."

"I know. I just need some time," Hannah replied. *Don't start, Robin.*

"Okay, no pressure. Just praying for you to experience the greatest love you could ever know."

"I know," Hannah said, not knowing what else to say. She still wasn't sure if she could experience the same relationship with God as Robin and Ms. Priscilla.

"Anyway, do you want to have a late lunch and maybe catch a movie? Michael has a training all day, so I was hoping we could hang out. Plus, this beginning of the school year stuff is going to make me loopy," Robin said.

"Girl, for real! After three years of teaching here, and it being the same info, I wish they would just send that stuff in an email."

"Right, and this is only my second year. I feel burned out already. I love my kids, but all of this paperwork is torture," Robin added.

"Well, hanging out sounds good."

"Alright. Let's do it."

"Okay. Now, let me get out of here," Hannah said.

"Okay."

"I'll call you once I'm done at the salon. Start thinking about where you want to eat," Hannah said, embracing her friend.

"Do you want to pick me up on the way leaving the salon, or do you want to park at my house, and I drive?"

"I may have to take you up on the driving part," Hannah stated, continuing up the hall.

"Oh, by the way, how are you feeling? We've been so stressed the last two weeks I forgot to ask," Robin inquired.

Hannah turned to face her. "I'm good."

"Well, take it easy."

"I will," Hannah replied.

"Alright now."

"Okay, see you tomorrow, girl," Hannah yelled over her shoulder as she turned and headed out the side door of the fourth-grade wing, admiring the student work displayed near the exit. She stepped outside and headed over to her car. *This heat is so disrespectful.* She unlocked the doors, threw her bag onto the backseat and placed her purse on the front passenger seat. Hannah then took out her cell phone and turned on the Bluetooth. She located her audiobook, wanting to drown out her thoughts about her relationship with her mother. She continued Redeeming Love by Francine Rivers. She had been listening to it off and on all week. It reminded her somewhat of her life. The woman in the story didn't feel wanted or worthy, so she continued in her self-destructive ways. In spite of her behavior, the man still loved her and continued to try to show her the way and save her from herself. Hannah had surely been destructive in her late teens, and she still felt unwanted and unworthy more often than she could count. She was surrounded by love, yet she longed for the love of her mom. As the book boomed through the car speakers, Hannah placed her phone in the opening under the dashboard. She then pulled out of the parking lot and headed toward home.

Maybe I should just call her, Hannah thought.

Remembering that she needed to grab a few items from the store, she pulled into the Food Mart just passed the school and ran inside, anxious to get home and rest. Hannah quickly grabbed a few necessities and some breakfast sausage. She would make a quick meal in the morning before they both headed out. *We've been eating out way too much,* Hannah thought as she paid for the items and headed outside. As she neared her car, Hannah saw Anton, a teacher from her school. They had also attended Clayton State together. Hannah laughed as she remembered their one date. After that, they both realized they should remain friends, and they had.

Anton and his family were parked a few rows down from her car. As they loaded their groceries, he spotted Hannah, smiled and waved. She returned the gesture. His wife was getting on to their daughter, who was being disrespectful. Hannah had seen his daughter in action one day passing the fifth-grade hall. She was telling her teacher what she wasn't going to do. When Hannah tried to pull her aside and talk to her, she had an attitude, so Hannah sent her back into the classroom. Hannah never mentioned it to Anton, not knowing how he would respond. She diverted her eyes, trying not to appear nosey. *I see she is a handful with her parents, too,* Hannah thought climbing into her car.

Minutes later, she pulled her black late-model Toyota Camry into the garage of their Forest Park townhome. Hannah was home before Levi as usual. Grabbing her purse and bag, she headed inside. Because it was Friday, Levi would normally pick something up for them on his way in.

Hannah headed up to their bedroom and into the master bath for a quick shower. After finishing, she threw on some pajama bottoms and a t-shirt, went into the living room and turned on their flat-screen television over the fireplace. *The Cosby Show.* Hannah loved to watch re-runs of these old shows. Halfway into the show, Hannah couldn't stop thinking about her mom. She decided to go ahead and call her.

She closed her eyes, attempting to calm her rapidly beating heart. Fingering the heart-shaped pendant on her silver necklace and taking another deep breath, Hannah picked up her cell phone, located her mom's number and pressed the call button. Her hands trembled as she awaited her voice.

"Hello," her mom spoke.

"Hey, Mama. This is Hannah."

"What?" her mom replied.

Hannah felt her heart rate increase. "I was just calling to see how you've been."

"Really? You decide to call me now?" Her mom's words were slurring.

"Mama, I just want us to have a talk and build a better relationship."

"We're talking now."

"Can I come by and see you one Saturday?"

"Why? Youve been over there with your sorry daddy and his family all these years, and you haven't even thought to come see me."

"Are you serious right now?" Hannah snapped. "Why do you do that?"

"Who are you raising your voice at?"

"I'm not raising my voice. I just don't understand why you treat me the way you do."

"Ain't nobody treating you like nothing."

"You've blamed me for what that dog Aunt Loretta is married to did to me when I was a young girl. You even treated me bad when I lived with you."

"That man ain't did nothing. Why do you keep lying? You were fast around my guy friends and my husband too before he skipped out."

"Mama, I was molested by Malcolm, and your boyfriends tried to push up on me a few times when I lived with you. What have I done for you to treat me so bad? What has made you so bitter?"

"You know what...I'm ain't doing this."

"Mama, why don't you love me?" Hannah asked, wiping away streams of tears.

"Girl, don't call me with this mess."

"Why won't you answer me, Mama?"

"I said, don't call me with this mess."

"I just thought we could try to fix things," Hannah stated.

"Ain't nothing to fix. You chose your daddy."

"What are you talking about? Both of you are my parents. I love both of you the same."

"I doubt that. You have glorified that man since I can remember, but he walked away from us, then you found a way to make your way over there with him."

"Is that what you believe?" Hannah asked, rubbing her temple, attempting to massage away the piercing headache that had come on suddenly.

"That's what I know."

"Mama, I have to go now. I want you to know that I do love you, and I hope you can love me someday too," Hannah stated before hitting the end button.

She placed her phone on the mocha-colored coffee table and lay back on the oversized, brown leather sectional. Hannah regretted making the call. As more tears flowed, she hated that rejection had once again invaded her space like an uninvited guest. Hannah closed her eyes and leaned back. Unable to focus on anything else and not wanting her mom's words to continue replaying in her mind, she soon drifted off to sleep.

Hannah was awakened by the beeping of the alarm system as Levi entered through the garage door. She sat up, her head still throbbed a little but not as bad as before falling asleep. Levi had bought Chinese. Hannah was starving. She stood and followed him into the kitchen, taking out the paper plates and forks. Hannah didn't feel up to washing any dishes, and she was sure Levi didn't either.

"I'm going to take off this uniform. Give me a minute, he stated.

"Okay."

"I'll just be a few minutes," he replied and kissed her on the cheek.

Her stomach growling, Hannah couldn't wait to dig in. She grabbed two paper plates and placed fried rice, sweet and sour chicken and an egg roll on each. She then grabbed two bottles of water from the fridge. Moments later, Levi walked in and sat at the island. As they ate, Hannah thought about the conversation with her mom. Now that she was going to be a mother herself, she wanted to mend her and her mom's broken relationship.

"You seem deep in thought. What's on your mind?" Levi asked.

"It's nothing."

"Yes, something is bothering you. Spit it out."

"Well, I–I tried calling Mama today, and it didn't go well."

"What do you mean?"

"Just the same ole stuff she's been saying for years. She thinks I wanted to go live with Daddy, so she says I lied about what Malcolm did to me. I was twelve, Levi. That was out of my control. Why didn't she get herself together, instead of blaming Daddy?"

"Babe, I know you love your mama, but I don't know why you want to put yourself through more stress. You did nothing wrong. Your mama has to come around, not you."

"I know. I just hoped we could mend all of this craziness. Brittany said she's still talking bad about me and Daddy."

"That's not cool. Why does Brittany keep bringing that nonsense to you?"

"I don't know."

"Why doesn't your mama try? Why doesn't she call you, Hannah? She has more than two kids. I get so angry when I think about what you've been through with her."

"I know, but Mama is going to be a grandmother, so I just thought it might be good for the baby to get to know her."

"I know, but I just don't want you stressing out about this. You've been disappointed so many times by her. I'm not sure I want my child around her after how she's treated you."

"Levi, I still want her to know her grandchild."

"I do, too, but I'm not putting up with nonsense when it comes to my child. I just want you to rest and stop worrying."

"I still want to work things out with Mama."

"Just take it easy, Hannah. You're only 12 weeks along."

"I just want things to be better between me and her."

"She has to want the same thing, babe."

Hannah looked at Levi, not knowing what to say after that. He was right, but it didn't make her feel any better. Changing the subject, she and Levi chatted about the baby and the craziness at his job while they ate. Levi and Hannah both smiled as they talked about the house being a little noisier soon. Hannah was grateful for him and his love for her. He took her hands, lifting the left one to his lips, kissing it tenderly. She gazed into his eyes as he stood and walked toward her. Pulling her from her chair, Hannah melted in her husband's embrace. She remained there for several minutes. Holding her, he whispered, "You are the best thing that's ever happened to me. You are going to be an amazing mother. You are not someone's throwaway. You did nothing wrong. I pray your mama will come around so she can get to know the great person you turned out to be."

Hannah could remain in his arms forever.

If only everything in my life was as perfect as this moment. If only Mama's heart would change.

If only...
Only time will tell.

CHAPTER TWO

Saturday, August 15

Hannah's alarm buzzed the next morning at 6:30. She had to be at the salon by 8:00, so she threw on some joggers and a t-shirt and pulled her natural, thick, curly hair back into a ponytail. She was getting a wash and trim today, which meant her hair had to be pressed out. Hannah sighed, realizing that would take an eternity. After finishing her hair and adding a little makeup and lip gloss, she lifted her top, admiring her belly. She only had a slight bulge in her stomach but still smiled with anticipation.

"I can't wait until you start growing more," Hannah said as she stared into the mirror, thinking about how the new baby and Levi were the only joys in her life at the moment. Of course, her dad was still at the top of her list, but with work, she didn't get to see him nor her aunt and uncle as much. She made a mental note to call and check on them later.

After daydreaming a few more minutes, Hannah walked back into their bedroom to wake Levi. He had to be at work by 8:30 on the other side of town.

Hannah headed into the kitchen to prepare some sausage, eggs and toast. She cut up the sausage and placed them in the oven and started straightening up around the house a little. She then sat down and turned on the T.V. There was a minister, Leah Murray, speaking on Lifetime. Hannah leaned back and listened. The topic was trusting God in the hard times. It intrigued her. She had definitely been through some rough patches in life.

The minister spoke. "Some people have done a disservice to many believers. They may make you believe that the struggle and pain you endured in the past was your fault or that God was punishing you. Some of you may believe that's why some things happened to you. That's just not true. You have to realize that your pain is tied to your purpose. God will work it all together for your good. I'm a living witness. Yes, it happened. We live in a fallen world. Satan uses people just as God does. God brought you through it. You may not even be saved, but God still loves you. Some of you may even be mad at God for what happened in your life, but he wants to deliver you from all of it so he can use you for his glory. Most of all, he wants you to know that his love for you is unsearchable."

As she stared at the screen, Hannah was reminded again of her past. For years, she did everything she could to not think about it. She got up the nerve to tell Levi back in college, but she begged him never to bring it up again, and he hadn't. However, she'd made the mistake of trying to reconnect with her mom. After talking to her mom and Brittany yesterday and listening to the minister on the screen now, Hannah tried all she could to push back her memories, but flashes of Malcolm came to her mind. Hannah's eyes filled with tears again. For years, she believed that God was angry with her, often wondering why he didn't stop those things from happening.

Hannah attempted to focus on the present. She was happy now with her husband and at least being able to see and talk to her siblings. *I don't want to relive any of it anymore,* Hannah sighed. The speaker's words had lured her to a place she hadn't intended to revisit ever again. Hannah understood that evil did exist; she had seen it in her aunt's husband as a kid, but there were times she just couldn't comprehend how a loving God could allow her to go through such pain. Ever since she was a little girl, she knew in her heart that there was someone greater, but she still struggled believing God loved her at times.

Hannah had accepted Christ into her life as a teen. She'd loved church back then and would attend every Sunday. Her dad and Aunt Melissa had taught her all about trusting in God, but the more she experienced over the years, the more she rejected church and guarded her heart against accepting God's love for fear of more disappointment. Robin and Ms. Priscilla had invited she and Levi to church more times than she could count. They had attended a few times, and Brittany had gone with them as well, but lately Hannah continued to make excuses as to why they couldn't make it. She knew Levi wanted the two of them to visit again, but he said he would stop pressuring her about it. At least twice a month, he attended his home church with his mom by himself.

After listening for a few more minutes, Hannah clicked off the television and went to the kitchen to scramble some eggs. She heard Levi talking on the phone. *Must be Mama Jefferson.*

After hearing the call end, Hannah turned to face Levi as he walked into the kitchen and kissed her softly on the lips.

"Good morning, husband," she whispered.

"Good morning, wife. I've got to eat quickly. I'm running late."

"Me too."

"Oh, yeah, Mama said hello."

"How's she doing?"

"She's doing better. Finally getting over that cold."

"Well, that's good."

"Yeah, I told her I'm coming by to see her tomorrow. You want to ride with me?"

"Tomorrow? Levi, you know I like to chill on Sundays. How about next Saturday?" Hannah replied as she prepared two plates and handed one to Levi.

"We can run by to see Mama and still chill once we get back home. She only lives ten minutes away."

"I know that. I wasn't planning to leave the house tomorrow."

"Okay. How about I run over to spend a few hours with her?"

"You know I don't have a problem with that," Hannah replied.

They both sat at the island to eat and chatted for a few minutes. After finishing up, Levi grabbed both plates and washed them before kissing her and dashing out the door.

Realizing she needed to speed it up, Hannah stood, grabbed her purse and headed out to the car. She was looking forward to the day of relaxation.

***

Finally finished at the salon, Hannah climbed into her car, grateful for the moment alone. She grabbed a tissue from the small pack she carried in her purse. She wanted the water works to stop. Hannah wasn't ready for the conversation she had just had with Ms. P. *I should be happy right now, not crying. I'm going to be a mother,* Hannah sighed.

Ms. Priscilla had taken Hannah to the back and prayed with her about the situation with her mom and for their new baby. Hannah just didn't get her mom's feelings towards her. So many years had passed. She sat for a moment, trying to calm herself. She checked her eyes in the rearview mirror. They were puffy and red. *Ugh.* She decided to drive around a bit to get herself together before heading over to Robin's, not wanting to spoil their girls' day out.

After arriving at her friend's house twenty minutes later, they climbed into Robin's car and were on their way. They finally decided on RJ's Barbecue Pit. It was a fairly new establishment in the Queen Street Shopping Plaza, just up the street from Ms. Priscilla's shop. The plaza had all the major retail stores and the enormous Christian bookstore that Robin and Ms. Priscilla always bragged about. In a better mood, Hannah admired the women moving about. They looked to be enjoying themselves, hanging out with their girlfriends. *Maybe that's why this area is called Queen Street,* Hannah thought. *Women from different ethnic backgrounds are always swarming this place.*

After circling the parking lot a few times, Robin found a space near the front. They climbed out of Robin's gold Honda Accord and headed inside.

"Girl, it's HAWT out here!" Robin said, waving her imaginary fan.

"Yes, it is. Let's hurry inside," Hannah replied, shaking her head, grinning at her friend.

As they stepped inside of the restaurant, they found a buzzing crowd. People were enjoying conversations all around. Hannah started to complain, but she remembered it was Saturday and realized it was the lunch rush. The hostess came over and asked how many were in their party.

"Just us," Robin replied.

"Okay, it will be at least a twenty-minute wait," the hostess stated, grabbing a clipboard to take down their names. Hannah was hungry, but she knew the wait time would fly by. She was surely not going back out there in that Georgia heatwave. She loved living here but had never enjoyed the summer months. It was August, and she still felt as if her skin would melt like wax on most days. Hannah couldn't wait until October. Then, at least, they would have some relief.

Hannah and Robin walked over and sat on the brown cushioned bench in the lobby area. She and Robin chatted for a few moments, admiring the new artwork, which didn't seem to fit in the barbecue joint. Sometime later, they were taken to their booth at the back of the restaurant.

"Your waitress will be here in a moment," the hostess stated before returning to her post up front.

"Girl, people love this place," Robin stated.

"Me, too," Hannah retorted.

"So how are you feeling today?"

"I'm good, just a little tired is all."

"Make sure you monitor that," Robin stated.

"Okay."

"We have to take care of ourselves. We're always doing for everyone else."

"That's for sure."

"Hello, ladies. I'm Ayana. What can I get you to drink to get you started?" the waitress asked, interrupting their conversation.

"Oh, how are you?" Robin asked, smiling. "You must be new. I haven't seen you before."

"Yes, I am. I started a few days ago. Now, what would you like to drink?" Ayana repeated as Hannah admired her beautiful sisterlocks neatly curled as she brushed them back across her slender shoulders.

"*Ummm,* can I have a sweet tea?" Robin asked.

"Sure, and you, ma'am?" the waitress asked, turning to Hannah.

"I'll take a lemonade."

"Sure thing. I'll get those right out to you. Do you ladies need a few more moments to look over the menu?"

"Yes," Hannah replied, remembering that they had been chatting and only half viewing it.

"Okay, I'll grab your drinks and be right back."

"Okay. By the way, your sisterlocks are gorgeous. Who did them? I wonder if I would ever be brave enough to lock my hair," Hannah stated.

"Thanks. I actually got them done at Natural Glory, the shop a few doors down from here."

"Oh, really?"

"Yeah. Patrice is amazing, but I do love your hair the way it is. It's so thick."

"Thanks," Hannah stated, rubbing her hands through her freshly pressed out, jet-black hair. "I just got it pressed. It only lasts for about two weeks, then it's back to my curls. I love the health of my hair, but it is not easy to manage all the time."

"I bet. Well, let me grab your drinks," Ayana replied, hurrying away, but was stopped by another waiter.

"They are working up in here," Robin said.

"Yes, they are. I remember my waitress job back in college. No joke," Hannah stated, noticing her stomach was growling. She started laughing and placed her hand over her belly as if the other patrons in the restaurant could hear it.

"What's funny?" Robin joined in.

"Girl, my stomach is growling. My child and I need some groceries real soon." Hannah continued laughing. Robin shook her head.

"You are a mess."

The waitress headed back over with their drinks and set the tray down on the table. She handed each of them their drink and took out her notepad from the pocket of her plaid apron.

"Okay, what are you ladies having today?"

"I'll have the barbecue leg quarter with baked beans and coleslaw," Hannah said quickly. The waitress then looked at Robin.

"I'll also have the barbecue leg quarter but with mac and cheese and coleslaw."

"I'll get that order right in for you ladies."

"Thank you," Hannah and Robin sang as the waitress hurried away again.

"Wow, she looks like she is about to pop," Hannah stated, looking at the pregnant woman taking a seat across from them. She wore the cutest pair of maternity ripped jeans with a flared green top.

"Oh, yes she does, but she is cute though."

"She is. I can't wait until my little one starts to really grow," Hannah said to her friend.

"It will be here sooner than you think."

"I know."

"So, what's up, other than us working like Hebrew slaves already and the school year just starting?" asked Robin.

"Nothing much. I tried calling my mama yesterday. It didn't go so well," Hannah said, her mood suddenly shifting.

"Oh. What happened?"

"She started going off about me choosing Daddy again and denying my abuse."

"That's crazy."

"I know. I just want to squash all of this drama in my family for the sake of my baby."

"It's drama you didn't cause, Hannah."

"I know, but I want to get over the things that went on back then."

"I agree, but have you really dealt with what happened to you and how your mom has continued to treat you over the years?"

"I've tried to forget about it, but it all came back to me this morning as I was listening to this minister on T.V., then I had a long conversation with Ms. P at the shop."

"Oh, really?"

"Yeah. I found myself sobbing."

"I'm sorry, friend."

"Thanks. Ms. P has me really thinking about what she said. She said I have to give Mama and my past to God."

"I agree."

"I find that hard to do sometimes," Hannah admitted.

"What do you mean?"

"Nothing."

"Talk to me. You know I'm here for you."

Hannah hesitated for several minutes, then said, "I mean, I've been struggling with trusting God. I don't know what I believe anymore. I accepted him in my teens, but over the years, I think I've started blaming him for everything I've been through. "

"You know God isn't people, right?"

"Yeah, but I just keep wondering why he let me go through so much hurt. And Mama's hatefulness toward me.

"God gave people a free will. He is not people. He loves you."

"I don't know."

"I do know. He never said life wouldn't happen. We have to deal with those things before we can move passed them. He can help us move past them."

"That's what I was trying to do by contacting Mama."

"In order to get passed something, you have to address it, not just pretend it didn't happen, and it doesn't sound like your mama is ready to address anything."

"I think I just need to try to reconnect with her. Maybe she will eventually come around. I don't have to deal with Aunt Loretta or Malcolm anymore."

"Didn't you just say how rude she was to you? She has to be willing to address things."

"I know, but Mama was drinking a lot back then. Still is."

"Yeah, but she isn't drinking 24/7. You can't be the only one trying."

"Well, maybe I'll try talking to her again. Maybe, I should just go see her. She would have no choice but to listen to me."

"That might not be the best idea right now. Focus on you and the baby."

"I've gotta keep trying."

"I'm gonna keep you and your family in my prayers. Prayerfully things will work out," Robin replied.

"I hope so," Hannah stated, rubbing her belly, giving Robin a half grin, not mentioning the light cramps she felt. They lasted a few minutes then went away.

Hannah and Robin hung out at the restaurant for another hour. They chatted about so much—from their childhood to their teaching careers. Deciding against the movies, they headed to check out the stores, starting with the Christian bookstore across the street. Hannah loved to read; it was one of her favorite pastimes.

"Have you read any Christian fiction?" Robin asked as they headed up the sidewalk, away from RJ's.

"I read a variety of fiction. I really like romance novels. I'm listening to this book by this lady, Francine Rivers. I'm enjoying it. It's called *Redeeming Love*. She's giving the guy a run for his money."

"Oh, that's one of her old ones. I've read that one. I love her books. She is definitely a Christian author," Robin stated as they walked toward the bookstore.

Hannah always admired the architecture of the red brick and crown molding on the buildings when she visited the area. She also loved how the owners maintained the grounds.

"I love the red brick," Robin stated.

"Are you reading my mind or something?" Hannah asked with a smile.

"Great minds think alike."

"I guess so," Hannah said as they walked into the store. She rubbed her belly, trying to ease another cramp.

"Are you okay?" Robin asked with a concerned look.

"Yes, I'm good."

"Are you sure? Do we need to head home?"

"No, I'm fine," Hannah assured Robin.

"Okay, then let's check out this joint and head over to Ross and T.J. Maxx."

"Oh, that's down my alley right there," Hannah replied, hoping everything was okay with the baby.

CHAPTER THREE

Sunday, August 16

After Robin had hounded her yesterday, Hannah decided to attend Robin and Ms. Priscilla's church again this morning. She now lay in bed trying to focus on the Lifetime movie on the flat-screen T.V. that sat on the mahogany wooden stand in the corner of their master bedroom. Levi had made it back from visiting Mama Jefferson and was downstairs watching T.V.

Hannah rubbed her belly, concerned about the cramps she continued to feel. They began to increase at church, and she did all she could to keep a smile on her face, but now she was really starting to worry. She didn't want to trouble her husband, so she tried to fight through and remain in bed.

"Babe, are you okay?" Levi asked, entering the room.

"Yes. I'm good."

"Are you sure? You're frowning. Are you in pain or something?" he asked, walking closer to their king-sized bed.

"Yeah. It's just a few cramps."

"Cramps? What do you mean? Is it your stomach?"

"Yeah, but it should be okay," Hannah stated, not sure if she was trying to convince Levi or herself.

"*Ummm,* how long have you been having these cramps?" Levi asked with a concerned look.

"Since yesterday."

"Why didn't you tell me?"

"I didn't feel like I needed to. I should be fine."

"Well, if they get any worse, I'm taking you to the emergency room."

"I have an appointment coming up. I'll just rest," Hannah said softly, rubbing her stomach again. *I hope everything is fine*, Hannah thought, her heart pounding as fear crept into her mind.

"Babe, you don't look fine."

"Levi, I'll let you know if it gets any worse."

"Okay. I'm watching the game. I'll be back up to check on you in a few," Levi stated, now standing in the doorway.

"Okay," Hannah replied, turning toward the T.V. as he stood there watching her. She felt another cramp but tried not to show it. "Levi, I'm okay. Go ahead and finish watching the game."

After he walked out, Hannah rubbed her stomach even more as the cramps continued. After they went on for a few more minutes, she began to fear the worse. She looked up at the ceiling and said a silent prayer, *I know we haven't been on really good terms, but I pray there is nothing wrong with my baby. Can you please protect him or her?*

After her prayer, Hannah tried to pay attention to the movie. She stretched out and turned on her side, placing a pillow under her belly. Just as she was getting somewhat comfortable, her cell phone rang. Thankfully, it was beside her. She turned it over and looked at the number. It was Aunt Melissa.

"Hello," Hannah whispered.

"Hey, sweetheart. How are you?"

"Okay, I guess, Auntie. I've been getting a few cramps in my stomach."

"Are they bad?"

"No, but I'm starting to worry a little."

"Everything is going to be fine. You probably just need to rest."

"You're probably right. This was a busy week at work with so much paperwork and meeting after meeting, and I was out with Robin yesterday. I probably just overdid it. I have an appointment in a few days."

"Okay. Just try to relax until then, but if they continue, have Levi take you to the ER."

"Okay."

"Where's Levi?"

"He's in the living room watching football."

"Well, tell him I said hello."

"I will. *Ummm.*" Hannah grunted, attempting to rub away the sharper pain she felt.

"Are you okay? Was that another cramp?"

"Yes, but it's easing off now."

"You do sound like you're hurting."

"Yeah, but it's getting a little better now," Hannah said, still trying to sound convincing but growing more and more afraid.

"Well, I'm going to pray right now. 'Dear, Heavenly Father. We come to you this evening on Hannah and Levi's behalf. Lord, I pray that you will touch Hannah right now, removing all of the pain. I pray that they will have a healthy child that will live to glorify you. Remove all worry from Hannah, and help her to trust you, not just with the baby in her womb but with her life. Thank you, Father, for loving Hannah and being with her. In Jesus' name. Amen. Now, call me if you need me," Aunt Melissa stated.

"Okay, I will. Where's Uncle Joseph?"

"He is in front of that T.V., as usual."

"Well, tell him I said hello. Hopefully, Levi and I can come out and see you all soon."

"You know we would love to have you, but you stay there and rest for now. We may get together with your daddy and come out there to hang out with you young folk soon."

"That would be great."

"Alright. We love you, and tell Levi we love him as well."

"I will. Love you, too, Auntie."

Placing her phone on the nightstand, Hannah shifted and sat up with her back to her pillows. She thought about Aunt Melissa for a moment. *I'm so thankful for her and Uncle Joseph being in my life. I still missed Mama growing up, but they made it a little easier.* After reflecting how amazing her dad's brother and his wife had been over the years, she felt more cramps. Not wanting to take any chances, she picked up her phone again to call her assistant principal and let her know she wouldn't be in tomorrow. Hannah told her where her sub folder was located on her desk and hung up.

A few minutes later, Levi walked back into their bedroom.

"How are you feeling?"

"My stomach is hurting more now."

"What's your doctor's number?"

"It's in my phone. I'll call her emergency line," Hannah replied, pulling up the number.

"Leave a message letting her know I'm taking you to the ER."

"Okay," Hannah stated, her shoulders tightening as she waited for the after-hours operator to pick up.

"Let me grab my shoes," said Levi, walking into the closet.

After leaving a message with the operator, Hannah lay there for a few more minutes as Levi waited to help her out of bed.

"Babe, I'll be right back. Let me use the restroom before we head out."

"Okay," replied Hannah. Terrified, she closed her eyes and prayed again, then, she stood and walked over to the dresser, pulling out a pair of her loose joggers and a t-shirt. Feeling more cramps, Hannah held her belly. She sat on the edge of the bed waiting for Levi to come out of the bathroom. Soon, the door opened, and she stood to go inside and get dressed.

"Anymore cramping?"

"Yes, a little," Hannah replied before closing the bathroom door.

As she used the restroom, a sharper cramp moved across the center of her stomach. Her heart raced when she saw light bleeding. Hannah grabbed a pad from under the sink, put it on, and began to get dressed. Tears began to flow. She sat on the side of the tub for several minutes, crying, her mouth covered with a towel. "Please don't let my baby die," Hannah spoke softly into the air. "Please, God. Please don't take him or her away from me. I've gone through enough," Hannah pleaded.

After getting dressed, Hannah headed back into the bedroom. Her heart ached as she watched her husband sitting on his side of the bed, his head in his hands. Seconds later, he looked up. Hannah noticed the tension on his face. He stood and walked toward her.

"Do you need me to help you with anything?"

"Can you grab my flats out of the closet?"

"Okay. You sit down."

"Okay," Hannah replied, taking a seat on the bed.

Just then, her cell phone rang. She stood, grabbing it off the nightstand. It was Dr. Sarin. Hannah answered as Levi reentered the bedroom and stood beside the bed. Hannah put the phone on speaker.

"Hi, Dr. Sarin."

"Mrs. Jefferson, how are you?"

"Not good. I think something is wrong."

"Tell me what's going on."

"Well, I started cramping yesterday when I was out with my friend. Now, I have some light bleeding."

"Okay."

"What should I do?" Hannah asked, her heart racing.

"Some women do have light bleeding during their pregnancy. Is your husband there with you?"

"Yes," Hannah and Levi replied at the same time.

"Please take her over to the ER. Tell them what's going on, and they will get her back immediately. We want to play it safe."

"Okay," said Levi. Hannah felt that her heart was in her throat. She didn't know what to say.

"Alright, let's remain positive. I'll see you for a follow-up on Tuesday. I'm hoping this is just a cervical polyp."

"What's that?" Hannah asked feeling hopeful.

"It is a harmless growth on the cervix, which could bleed during pregnancy due to higher estrogen levels."

"I hope so too," said Hannah.

"Hang in there, sweetie," Dr. Sarin said before hanging up.

Placing her phone on the bed, Hannah stood. Levi wrapped his arms around her. She couldn't calm her nerves. They were just excited a few nights ago about becoming parents. Now, she feared the worse.

"Let's head to the car," Levi said.

"I'm scared."

"I am too, but we have to believe that everything is okay."

"I really hope so," Hannah stated.

"Everything will be okay," Levi said. He then grabbed her hands and began to pray.

"Lord, please hear my prayer. I pray for my child and my wife. Please..."

As Levi continued to pray, Hannah's heart pounded. She tried to focus, but her mind raced. Once he was done, Levi helped her down the stairs, rushed into the kitchen to grab his keys, and they made their way to the car.

Climbing into the car, Hannah and Levi made their way to the hospital. Once they arrived, Levi ran inside to grab a wheelchair. As he helped her into the chair, Hannah felt more cramps coming on. She gripped Levi's hand, afraid to go inside.

"Babe, we have to get you checked out."

"I know. I'm scared. The cramps are increasing."

"I'm here for you. Let's get you inside."

As they entered, Levi rolled her over to the nurses' station. Hannah was once again at a loss for words, so Levi explained what she was experiencing. Hannah searched the nurse's eyes for a sign of hope.

This can't be happening.

As Levi filled out the paperwork, another nurse appeared and rushed Hannah into the back and began taking her vitals. She sat, staring at the pale walls, wondering if this was all a dream and wanting desperately to be awakened.

CHAPTER FOUR

Monday, August 17

Hannah and Levi arrived home in the wee hours of the morning after being at the hospital for several hours. After her vitals were taken, she was moved to a room. A few hours later, the cramps increased even more. The nurse had given her meds to relieve the pain. After an ultrasound, she was told her worse fear. She had miscarried their first child.

Aunt Melissa, her dad and Brittany had come to the hospital and remained there until she was released. Hannah was grateful for their presence.

Exhausted, they both climbed out of the car and went inside. Hannah wondered what Levi was feeling. She didn't know what to say. *What if he blames me? Maybe I somehow caused the miscarriage. Maybe I worried too much about me and Mama.* Her mind raced.

Levi opened the front door and allowed her to pass. She walked into the living room and plopped down on the couch, kicking off her shoes. Levi placed his keys on the table over by the door, then came and sat beside her. Nervous about what he would say, Hannah reached for the TV remote. Levi placed his hand over hers before she could click the On button. He shifted to face her.

"Babe, we've got to talk."

"I know," Hannah whispered, looking down.

"When I was young, I used to hear my parents argue because Mama said Pops didn't like talking. As I got older, I watched their relationship get stronger because they began talking more. Mama once got on to me about holding in stuff. She said it wasn't healthy."

"I don't know what to say. I mean, one minute we're expecting, and the next minute, I'm miscarrying. What did I do wrong?"

"Hannah, it's not your fault."

"How do you know that? Maybe I stressed to much about that craziness with Mama."

"Babe, stop it. Don't do that to yourself. You know how much I blamed myself for Pop's heart attack. I drove myself crazy because we had argued before he died."

"I remember. I thought Mama Jefferson was going to have to hurt you."

"Mama knows what's up," Levi said, laughing.

"Thank you! You are always trying to make me feel better," said Hannah, eyeing her husband.

"Babe, we're going to get through this together."

"I never thought I..." Hannah's stumbled.

"Neither of us thought you would miscarry. It's hard, but life happens sometimes."

"This is the hardest thing I've ever experienced."

"Me too. Again, we'll get through this together."

"I hope so."

"We will. I love you," Levi replied, wrapping his arms around her.

"I love you too."

"Alright. Let's get some rest."

"I'll try."

They both stood and headed upstairs. Levi was out before his head hit the pillow good. Hannah stared up at the ceiling, thinking about the short time she had carried her baby. Tears streamed down her cheeks as she searched her mind for what could have gone wrong. *How could things change so fast?*

After tossing and turning for several hours, Hannah was unable to rest. She kept seeing herself holding her baby in a dream and couldn't stand it anymore, so she sat up and stared at the ceiling, thinking about what she had endured in a matter of hours. Hannah looked at the clock on her nightstand. It flashed 6:33 a.m. She sat there a few more minutes, staring off into space. Levi still slept, so Hannah decided to go into the living room and stretch out on the couch. After slowly making her way downstairs, she shifted from one end of the couch to the other. Then after changing the channel over and over, Hannah finally saw the sun peeking through the living room blinds. Her eyes drooped as she continued to fight off sleep, not wanting to be reminded of their ordeal. She soon lost the battle and finally drifted off to sleep.

Sometime later, Hannah jumped up to the sound of her alarm clock. She clicked the T.V. remote to check the time. Now 8:00 A.M., she decided to try to cook something to eat. Before going into the kitchen, she got up and headed upstairs to turn off the alarm, realizing Levi had attempted to but had pressed the wrong button.

He must be exhausted. He's still knocked out, Hannah thought, looking at her husband stretched out across the bed.

As she headed out of the bedroom, she remembered that Brittany had promised to come by later today. She had a few more hours before being forced to hold a conversation. Hannah just didn't feel up to it.

Walking into the kitchen and searching for something quick to prepare, she suddenly felt sad. She felt as if a precious jewel had been ripped from her womb without the opportunity to realize its value. Hannah thought it was all a cruel joke and imagined what their child would have looked like. *I will never know now.*

"It's just not fair!" Hannah spewed. "I never asked for this. Why have all of these things happened to me? Am I being punished for something? I prayed to you. Aunt Melissa prayed to you. Ms. Priscilla prayed to you. Levi prayed to you, but my child still died. And not to mention how my mother has never wanted to be a part of my life. And did you forget, I was violated, and my aunt Loretta never seemed to want any part of me after that? Now this! What did I do in my life that was so bad?" Hannah wailed.

Not realizing that Levi was awake, Hannah was startled when he came rushing into the kitchen. She was too embarrassed to look at him. Her husband wouldn't be a father now thanks to her. Hannah was sure it was something that she had done wrong. Levi wrapped his arms around her, and she buried her face in his chest. Seconds later, she looked at him and began to apologize again. He placed his finger on her lips.

"It's not anybody's fault, Hannah. I love you, no matter what."

"What are we going to do, Levi? This really hurts."

"It's going to be okay. Take a drive with me to get something to eat."

"I don't want to go anywhere."

"Babe, come on. Just go with me. You have to try to keep a good headspace."

"I'll try."

"Okay. Now, go throw on some clothes and come on. I don't want to leave you to your thoughts."

"I'm supposed to stay inside, remember?"

"You don't have to get out. We can sit in the car and eat, then drive around. I don't want to leave you."

"I'm not going to be good company."

"Yes, you will."

***

"Alright, let's find something to watch on Netflix," Levi stated later that morning, trying to keep her spirits up.

"I really don't feel up to watching a movie."

"Come on. I'll let you choose."

"I'm not up to it."

"Well, you're stuck with me, so we're going to just UNO it out. Let me go grab the cards. We might play a li'l Monopoly too."

"*Uhhh*, Levi?" Hannah called as he stood and jogged up the stairs and into the office.

Hannah didn't want to think about their lost, but she wasn't up to playing any games or watching any movies. She just wanted time to reverse, and she would still be carrying her child. As she waited for Levi to return, she scrolled through her Instagram page until she got to the picture of one of her co-workers holding her infant son. Hannah clicked out of her page and threw her phone down on the couch beside her. It then vibrated. She lifted it again. It was her dad. Hannah answered and clicked the speaker button.

"Hey, Daddy," Hannah mumbled.

"Hey, sweetheart. Just calling to check on you."

"I'm okay."

"You don't sound okay."

"I'm fine. Just trying not to think about the miscarriage," Hannah said as Levi came down the stairs, armed with games.

"We'll help you through this," her dad said.

"I know.

"When do you have to see the doctor?"

"I have a follow-up tomorrow. She'll let me know when I can go back to work."

"I think you need to take your time."

"Daddy, I need to take my mind off everything. I think seeing my kids will help me."

"I don't know. If you don't feel up to it, please let someone know before you try to drown yourself in your work."

"I will, Daddy," Hannah said, shaking her head and eyeing Levi. He nodded, agreeing with her dad.

"I plan to come out and spend the weekend with you on Saturday."

"Daddy, you don't have to do that."

"Come on, Pops," Levi chimed in.

"I guess you're outnumbered. My son-in-law said it's a go. Don't even try and talk me out of it."

"I won't. You know I want to see you."

"Good. Your aunt Melissa said she's coming out to visit you soon. She wanted to give you some time to rest."

"Okay. Tell Auntie and Uncle Joseph I love them and you."

"You know we love you, princess."

"Daddy, I told you I'm grown now. Why do you still call me that?"

"You can be one hundred and five and still be my princess."

"Thank you for checking on me. See you later, Daddy."

After hanging up, Hannah looked over at Levi sitting at the dining room table, shuffling the Uno cards. Hannah couldn't help but laugh at her husband.

"You are so crazy," Hannah said, standing.

"Oh yeah, I'm ready. Remember that time you cheated me out of UNO at our last family barbecue? It's on now."

Hannah smiled, "What am I going to do with you? You're determined to make me play this game."

"Facts. Let's go." Levi laughed, pointing to the chair.

Hannah took a seat. She waited for Levi to pass out the cards. Once he was done, he reviewed the rules, reading them from his cell phone screen. Hannah shook her head. She loved her husband's silly personality. She needed this because all she wanted to do was go upstairs, sit on the floor in their closet and cry.

An hour had passed, and Hannah had beat Levi a few times, even after he had attempted cheating by trying to get her to look away so he could hide some of his cards. He had made her feel better. For a moment, Hannah had taken her mind off of their loss. She thought back to their college days when they would play each other for who would buy lunch. They had become friends a year before they actually started dating.

Now, he sat before her. Her groom. This was Hannah's strong Black man. Only a year older than Hannah, she loved his distinguished look and walnut complexion. With his broad shoulders, low haircut, jet-black goatee and black, thick-rimmed glasses, he could've easily been mistaken for a young college professor. Hannah loved to see when he dressed in his polo shirts and Khakis for church or if they were going out to dinner or the movies.

As Hannah continued to stare at her husband, she wondered which of them their baby would have looked like.

"Babe, it's your turn," Levi stated, pulling her from her thoughts.

"Oh, I'm sorry. Is this our last game? I want to go take a nap."

"Yeah. We can stop after this. Let me whip you real quick."

"Whatever, man. Deal the cards," Hannah said, grinning.

As they got into the next game, the doorbell rang. Hannah wondered who that could be, then remembered that Brittany had told her she would be by. Hannah placed her cards on the table and got up to answer it. When she got to the door, Hannah could see Brittany's petite frame through the frosted glass. She opened the door and hugged her sister.

"Hey." Hannah smiled, pulling Brittany into an embrace.

"How are you feeling? I guess that isn't the best question under the circumstances."

"I'm doing a little better."

"I tried to call Malik, but he didn't pick up. I'll try him again later."

"That's okay. Hopefully, I'll get to talk to him soon. Come on in," Hannah said, leading Brittany through the living room. Brittany waved at Levi.

"How are you, li'l sis?" Levi asked.

"I'm good. How are you?"

"Doing okay, I guess."

"That's good."

"How's school?" Levi asked.

"Well, that nursing program is tough, but I'm determined."

"That's what I like to hear. Want to join us for a game of UNO?"

"No, I'm good."

"You sure you don't want to join in and get the same butt kicking I'm about to give your sister?"

"I'm good," Brittany said, laughing and shaking her head.

"A'ight. Maybe next time."

"Girl, don't mind my husband."

"I know my brother-in-law is crazy."

"I heard that," Levi said as Hannah led Brittany over to the couch.

"So, how are you, sis?" Brittany asked.

"I'm okay. Levi is helping me keep my mind occupied."

"That's good. Make sure you are getting some rest."

"There you go, sounding like a nurse already."

"I guess I am."

Hannah and Brittany sat and chatted for several minutes. Levi had gone into the garage. Because of the noise, Hannah assumed he was organizing the shelves he had installed.

"How many more courses do you have again?"

"Girl, it seems like a hundred."

"I bet. Then, you still have to do an internship."

"Don't remind me. I want to be a nurse, but I just wish it would speed up."

"Well, you only have this year and next year."

"I'm glad. I have lots of work to do right now. I just took a break to come and see you."

"Well, thank you, sister," said Hannah.

After hanging out for a few more minutes, Brittany stood to leave.

"I'm going to head out to get some more studying done."

"Okay. Thanks again for coming by," Hannah said, standing to hug Brittany again.

"Why wouldn't I," Brittany said. "Is there anything you need me to do? When are you going back to work?"

"Hopefully in a few days."

"Okay, well, let me know if you need anything."

"I will."

"And don't try to rush yourself. Sit down somewhere."

"Really?"

"Yes, really," Brittany said, laughing, wrapping her arms around Hannah. They held each other for several seconds before separating.

"Love you, sis."

"Love you too," Brittany said, wiping away a lone tear. "You take it easy."

"I'll try," Hannah stated, walking her sister to the door.

Once they got to the door, Hannah hugged her sister once again. She watched as Brittany climbed into her car. Hannah found herself shedding tears as Brittany pulled away. Each time they hung out together, Hannah enjoyed their laughter and getting to know each other more. She was grateful her sister had come and wished her mom was with her.

As she turned to head out to the garage, Hannah remembered what her aunt Melissa once told her, "You'll recognize those who are in your corner when you're at your lowest. They'll be the ones to show up." She smiled at the thought. Hannah's mind drifted to her mom. She wondered if she would ever have her in her corner. She wanted to share the news of the miscarriage with her but didn't know what her response would be.

Another wave of sadness washed over Hannah as she was reminded that she wouldn't get the opportunity to love her child unconditionally—something she had never experienced but had always longed for.

As she entered the garage, Levi was sitting in his car with his eyes closed. He hadn't heard her come in. She walked around to the other side of his car to get to the driver's seat. He had his earbuds in, listening to the sports radio app he loved. When she touched his shoulder, he jumped and wiped his eyes quickly. Hannah's heart sank. She hadn't seen Levi cry since his dad's funeral.

"I'm sorry," Hannah cried, wrapping her arms around his neck. He stood, wiping away another tear.

"I told you, it's not your fault. I love you."

"I love you too."

Standing in their garage in the August summer heatwave, Hannah and Levi held each other in silence. She soaked his gray Adidas t-shirt with her tears, and she was glad he had entrusted her with his as well.

CHAPTER FIVE

Tuesday, August 18

Following their loss, Hannah and Levi headed to Dr. Sarin's private office, housed in a beautiful red brick building near downtown Forest Park on Main Street. Hannah's stomach did backflips as they headed to the elevator. As if able to feel her anxiety, Levi placed his arm around her waist as he pressed the button to Dr. Sarin's floor. Hannah rested her head on his shoulder.

"It's going to be okay, sweetheart. We'll get through this together."

"I hope so."

"It's all going to work out. Once the doctor gives us the clearance, we can try again. God has given us each other, and we need his strength now more than ever before."

"Again? I don't even know how to get passed this."

"Together, that's how," Levi repeated as the elevator doors opened.

They stepped inside. Hannah continued holding on to her husband for dear life. They were silent on the way up to the third floor. The door opened moments later, and they headed down the hall. Dr. Sarin had been Hannah's doctor for years. She had received recognition recently for being the best ob-gyn in their area.

Levi held the door for Hannah to enter. There were a few women already waiting. Hannah was grateful that Dr. Sarin was the only doctor in her office. In her situation, she knew she needed as much stability as possible. She didn't want to be seen by anyone else. Hannah stepped to the desk to sign in. They were a few minutes early. Ms. Angela, the receptionist, always greeted her with a smile.

"How are you? What time was your appointment?"

"At 1:00 P.M."

"Okay."

"I'm here for a follow-up appointment."

"Oh, yeah. I remember talking to you briefly on the phone. How are you feeling under the circumstances?"

"As best I can, I guess," Hannah replied, nearing tears again.

Ms. Angela placed her hand on top of hers as she continued to sign the clipboard. She squeezed, and Hannah could feel her strength from that interaction. Ms. Angela handed her another clipboard, asking her to fill as much out as she could. Levi grabbed it instead. She was grateful. It was as if he knew what she was thinking. He seemed to understand that it would be difficult for her to answer any questions about the miscarriage. Hannah nodded and turned to take a seat. Levi sat next to her, filling out the form.

The door next to the receptionist's desk opened. A woman held a newborn wrapped in a pink blanket. Hannah stared. *I wonder if my baby was a boy or girl.* Hannah noticed the woman's tender interaction with the baby. The mother covered the baby's head and walked over to the desk. Hannah looked down at her empty hands then back up at the woman. She tried averting her eyes but couldn't. The woman must have felt her peering at her. Her eyes met Hannah's for a moment. Then, Hannah finally turned toward her husband. Levi grabbed her hand.

"Sweetheart, I know this is hard for you."

Hannah nodded at her husband and looked at the woman holding the infant one last time before she and the baby disappeared out the door.

Try again. Try again. Those words raced through her mind. They terrified Hannah. *What if I get pregnant and miscarry again? I won't be able to handle that.* She shifted in her seat and tried to focus on the T.V. screen. It was tuned into the local news. The screen flashed to a convenience store robbery in Atlanta. The police were able to arrest the suspects on the scene trying to escape, but their car had stalled. They all didn't look to be more than sixteen years of age. The anchor's voice cracked as she shared the condition of the store clerk. He had been shot in the head three times and remained in critical condition. Hannah was shocked at the boldness of the youth. She was reminded why she taught the younger grades. She wanted to reach them to instill a desire to be great at an early age.

One of the women waiting was called to the back. Hannah stared at her huge belly as she passed. She then turned to look at Levi again. He had nodded off to sleep. Hannah tapped him lightly on his knee. He stirred and smiled at her, gripping her hand tighter.

"When are you planning to return to work?" Hannah managed to ask.

"I think I'll go back tomorrow if you don't need me to stay at home longer."

"I was thinking about asking the doctor to clear me to go back tomorrow myself," Hannah revealed.

"Tomorrow? Sweetheart, why are you wanting to go back so soon?"

"Levi, we both have to go to work at some point and being with the kids will help me take my mind off our loss."

"You think going back to a classroom full of third graders will help you forget you just miscarried?"

"You don't understand, Levi. I enjoy teaching. My students make me laugh. I need that right now."

"Okay. Just promise me you'll allow me to be here for you," Levi stated, looking into Hannah's eyes.

"I promise," she said and turned her attention back to the television.

"Hannah Jefferson," the nurse called out as she stood in the doorway.

Hannah and Levi rose. He squeezed her hand once more before they headed to the back. The older African American nurse led them to the third room on the right. She asked Hannah to sit in the chair next to the counter. Levi took a seat by the door.

"How are you doing today?"

"Okay, I guess," Hannah replied.

"Well, my name is Nurse Maggie. I'm going to take your blood pressure and weight first."

"Okay. Are you new here?" Hannah asked.

"No. I work out at the Atlanta office most of the time."

"I knew I had never seen you," Hannah stated, removing her jacket. The nurse proceeded to take her blood pressure, recording the reading on the tablet in front of her. She then asked Hannah to step on the scale: 150 pounds. Hannah noted she was down three pounds since the last time she had checked her weight. She hated being reminded of how much she had gained since college. Hannah stepped down, and the nurse directed them to follow her down the hall. The nurse led them into exam room three, instructing Hannah to undress from the waist down. Nurse Maggie handed Hannah a gown from the drawer on the side of the bed. Levi grabbed a magazine from the counter and pulled the chair by the door next to the exam table.

"The doctor will be with you soon," the nurse said, looking at Hannah before closing the door.

Hannah undressed quickly, placing her folded clothes in the chair by the door. She climbed onto the exam table, looking around the room, scanning the different charts on the wall. Her eyes landed on a chart about what to do after a miscarriage. It had a number for support. She considered writing it down but decided against it. She wasn't so sure she needed to seek counseling. The door opening brought her back to the present.

"How are you, Hannah?" Dr. Sarin asked, walking closer to the exam table. The same nurse was behind her.

"I'm okay, I guess," Hannah said.

"I'm truly sorry for your loss. I know this isn't easy."

"It isn't. I just want to get passed it all," Hannah stated, eyeing her husband. He grabbed her hand again. Hannah was comforted knowing he was there.

"It won't be easy, dear. We respond to the healing process in different ways," Dr. Sarin explained.

"We?" Hannah questioned.

"Yes. I experienced a miscarriage several years ago. I was heartbroken."

"I never knew that."

"I know. I still don't like to talk about it. I mentioned it to you to encourage you."

"Encourage?"

"Yes. I was blessed with three more beautiful children after that."

"That is encouraging. I'm just scared that I'll miscarry again."

"That's a normal feeling."

"You experienced that too?"

"Yes, for some time."

"How did you get passed it?"

"When my oldest was born."

"Huh?"

"Yes. Once I made it to the last trimester with Zara, I had hope, and I didn't focus so much on the previous miscarriage."

"Thanks for sharing that."

"You're most welcome, dear," Dr. Sarin said, stepping closer and placing her hand on Hannah's shoulder. "You will get through this. You just wait and see."

"I hope so."

"In due time. You'll see. Alright now, go ahead and lie back. I'll be checking to assure you're healing well from the D&C done at the hospital." Dr. Sarin spoke as Hannah lay back on the table. The nurse handed Dr. Sarin the tools needed to complete the exam.

Hannah took a deep breath.

"Just relax," the nurse spoke softly. "This will be over soon."

Hannah winced from the excruciating pain in her abdomen as the doctor completed her exam. *Why is there so much pain?* She squeezed her eyes shut and shifted, attempting to push herself up using her elbows. "That really hurts."

"Remain still and take a deep breath, dear. I'm almost done," Dr. Sarin instructed.

The nurse assisted Hannah in laying back and placed her hand over Hannah's, trying to comfort her as tears began to flow. *What's wrong? Why is this hurting so bad?*

Hannah remembered her previous appointment before finding out she was pregnant. There was pain with that exam also, but she assumed it was normal. The pain was worse now.

A few moments later, Dr. Sarin was done. She instructed Hannah to sit up.

"Mrs. Jefferson, I'm going to have to do a laparoscopy to be on the safe side. It looks as if you're healing fine, but I'm concerned about some of the pain and the cause of the miscarriage."

"A what?" Hannah asked. She frowned and stared at the doctor, confused as to what she was talking about.

"It's an exam where I go through your belly button with a laparoscope, which is a tiny camera on what looks like a small pole. I use it to see what I may be unable to view on an ultrasound. I'll be looking at your ovaries, making sure they aren't blocked and operating properly," Dr. Sarin explained.

"Okay, I think." Hannah spoke softly, not sure what else to say.

"You've had some issues with your cycle long before the miscarriage, so I want to make sure there are no other issues going on. I had someone cancel, so I can do the procedure on Monday. We want to get it done as soon as possible anyway."

"Okay. When do you think I can return to work?"

"I wouldn't advise going back to work too soon. You may have to be out at least a few more days after the procedure on Monday. We don't want any infections to arise, and I would advise you staying at home a little longer."

"Days? I need to get back to my students." Hannah raised her voice, not knowing if she could be alone with her thoughts for that long, especially with Levi possibly having to go back to work.

"Hannah, you need to focus on healing, physically and emotionally. When we experience a miscarriage, we think we'll be okay, but there are long-term effects. I just want you to give it some time."

"Okay, okay. I get it," Hannah stated in frustration. Levi stood, rubbing her back.

"Babe, let's just take it one day at a time," Levi stated softly, handing her a tissue to dry her tears.

Dr. Sarin attempted to encourage her again before instructing her to get dressed, and the clerk would have the paperwork ready for her to sign, authorizing the procedure.

"Don't eat anything after midnight on Sunday evening. Also, the procedure will be done in the outpatient center of the hospital. My receptionist will give you the information," Dr. Sarin stated before exiting the room. Hannah sat for a minute, breathing in and out. She was trying to process all she had been told. She wanted to throw something. *What else? I'm tired of this. I just want to forget about all of this.*

A few minutes later, she was dressed, and they headed to the clerk's desk. After receiving the instructions about Monday's procedure, they headed to the car.

"I'll let my supervisor know so I can be there," Levi finally said.

"Thank you."

"You don't have to thank me. That's my job as your husband. You know I love you," Levi said, unlocking the car doors.

"I love you too," Hannah replied, glancing at him before she climbed onto the passenger seat.

Levi got in and started the car. She stared out the passenger window. Hannah felt Levi watching her. She didn't know what to say. *I hope he doesn't blame me.*

"You okay?" Levi asked.

"Yeah, I guess. I would love if Daddy could be there, too," she finally said.

"You can ask him. He might be able to get off."

"Let me call him."

Hannah let out a loud sigh and pulled her cell phone from her purse to call her dad as they pulled out of the parking lot. It rang three times before he picked up.

"Hi, sweetheart. What's up?" her dad spoke into the receiver.

"Hi, Daddy. I have to have a procedure on Monday, and I would love for you to be there with me if you can."

"I would love to be there, sweetheart. Let me ask my supervisor. It shouldn't be an issue. I have several days saved up. I'll call you back on my break and let you know. Do you mind if I ask Aunt Melissa to come as well? Us menfolk don't know what to do all the time, but she would be great."

"I would love that, Daddy. I know I need to get out there to see you all more."

"I spoke to your uncle Joseph the other day. He asked about you."

"Thanks for letting me know. I'll give Aunt Melissa a call myself. I did get to talk to her briefly yesterday."

"Alright. I have to get back to work. I'll call you back in a few hours."

"Okay," Hannah said before disconnecting the call. She shifted to look at Levi. He looked worried.

"Levi, are you okay?" Hannah asked.

"I'm good. I just want you to be okay. I'm praying for God to be with us."

"I just want everything to work out. I know we can be great parents," Hannah replied. "Oh yeah, Daddy is going to try to be there, and he mentioned asking Aunt Melissa to come too."

"Okay, cool."

"She has been great over the years. She has stood in when Mama wasn't there, and I'm not even her real niece."

"You say that a lot, but she and Unc have been married so long, you might as well be her's too. They're great people."

"Yes, they are. For the past few days, I've thought again about trying to mend mine and Mama's relationship," Hannah announced. "I wish I could talk to her. I love Auntie, but I would love if Mama could be with me at this time."

"I understand. I can't imagine not having my mama to talk to."

"I know. I wish I could have the kind of relationship with her that you and Mama Jefferson have. Is that too difficult for someone to ask their biological mom?"

"Not at all. Just remember, you're dealing with a lot right now. I don't want you to have any more disappointment."

"I guess you're right," Hannah said, speaking what she thought her husband wanted to hear. She then grew silent.

Hannah's mind drifted to a day when she was nine. That was a day she would never forget. Hannah was sick with a bad cold, and her mom allowed her to stay home from school. She had taken the day off as well. Malik and Brittany were at the babysitter, so her mom could tend to her. Hannah's mom had made her a cup of tea, lemon and honey. Hannah had loved the sweet taste of extra honey she had included to get her to drink it all down. Her mother then let her curl up next to her on the couch as she watched the soaps. Hannah had asked her mom a million questions that day. She had smiled and answered all of them. There was no frustration in her voice, no crude comments. Rejection was never a thought in Hannah's mind on that day. Because her mama was sober, Hannah experienced a joyful moment of peace and security. She wished she could call her now and that woman show up at her appointment to care for and be there for her on Monday. Hannah loved the woman she spent time with that day. Where had she gone? Would she ever return?

CHAPTER SIX

Monday, August 24

"There's a very slim chance of you conceiving anymore."

"What?" Hannah asked with a terrified glare.

Levi squeezed her hand to get her to relax. He leaned over and whispered in her ear, asking her to hear the doctor out. They were still at her outpatient appointment. Hannah and Levi had arrived at 6:00 A.M. The procedure was over, and Dr. Sarin was now explaining her findings from the laparoscopy. Hannah had been resting in recovery for a few hours waiting for the doctor to come in.

"Mr. and Mrs. Jefferson, the laparoscopy results show that Hannah's left ovary is covered by a large cyst, and both are covered with endometriosis," she explained, her eyes shifting from Hannah to Levi. Hannah couldn't believe what she was hearing. She tried hard to focus on the doctor's words.

"Wait. How did we get pregnant before? Doc, could you please explain what all this means?" Levi asked calmly.

"Well, I'll start with trying to answer your first question. Some women are able to get pregnant, but they have a high risk of miscarrying. Now to the other question. Cysts can grow during certain times of the month and shrink as well. However, endometriosis has to be removed. It can cause infertility."

"Where does this endome...whatever it's called come from?" Levi continued his round of questions.

"According to the current research, endometriosis occurs when the endometrium tissue that normally lines the uterus begins to grow outside of it. When this happens, it may cover the ovaries and other organs as well. Hannah has a large amount of it. This may need to be removed by performing a full or partial hysterectomy. This will be the last resort. Based on Hannah's pain during the exam at the office and during her previous cycles, this may possibly be our only resolution."

"Really?" Levi asked.

"Yes, unfortunately. However, before I go any further with that conversation, I'd like to recommend her to an infertility specialist first."

"Okay, what will they do?"

"They will offer the other treatments, and she will report to the specialist periodically for checkups and updates," explained Dr. Sarin. Hannah began to cry, her head in her hands.

"That's a plus. I am glad there are other treatments she can try," Levi said. Hannah was glad her husband was there and was hopeful because she was still trying to get passed the *slim chance of conceiving* statement.

"Yes, but they are not guaranteed."

"I don't care," Hannah finally spoke, looking up at Dr. Sarin, wiping away tears with the back of her hand. "I want to try one of the treatments before I make any other decision,"

"I think you should too. I just have to tell you the truth about your options. Just note, there is a large amount of endometriosis, so we want to try what we can as soon as possible. There is a risk that it can cover your bowels and bladder, and other organs."

"What would that do?" Hannah asked.

"It could cause more pain when you go to the restroom and other issues in the near future."

"Oh, I don't want that to happen," Hannah said. Levi stood quietly beside her, rubbing her hand.

"It can get very painful, but the specialist can give you more details and better inform you of the risks. I'm going to have the clerk get you the contact info for a few infertility specialists in our network."

"Okay, I do have another question," said Hannah. "Isn't there invitro or something like that? Can't we do that to conceive again, if needed?" Hannah asked.

"Oh, you mean in vitro fertilization?"

"Yes."

"That's an option, but it's not guaranteed either. It's where the specialist would collect your eggs and attempt to fertilize them with your husband's sperm. They would then implant the embryos in your womb. It can get very expensive. You can ask the specialist more about that option as well."

"Okay, but that may have to be one of our last options. We can't really afford anything really expensive. I want to try a treatment first," Hannah said, sighing and shaking her head, feeling as if she needed some air.

Levi wrapped his arms around her.

"Mr. and Mrs. Jefferson, I hate to be the bearer of more bad news, but I had to explain my findings. Sadly, an endometriosis diagnosis is all too common," Dr. Sarin said.

"How so?" Levi asked.

"It affects an estimated one in every ten women during their reproductive years between ages fifteen to about forty-eight or forty-nine."

"Wow," Hannah said.

"Mrs. Jefferson, again, I'm so sorry for your loss, and I wish I would've had a different report for you," Dr. Sarin said.

"Thank you," Hannah mumbled.

"Okay. Have a good day," the doctor finally said before exiting the room.

Hannah asked Levi to pass her clothes in the bag in the chair behind him. He helped her get dressed, and they headed into the lobby. Aunt Melissa and her dad sat watching television. Hannah walked pass as Levi stopped to talk to them. She moved in slow motion, heading to the double doors.

"Hannah, babe, wait up. You're going to hurt yourself."

"I just need a minute," she said over her shoulder.

"Hannah, please."

Hannah stopped and sat on a bench in the shade on the side of the hospital. She held her stomach.

"Are you in pain?" Levi asked.

"A little."

"Babe, you have to be careful. Let's head to the car."

"Just let me sit here for a minute."

"We need to get you home."

Levi grabbed her hand and pulled her up from the bench. She tried to push him away, but he held on to her. The waterworks began again. She was tired. She wanted happiness. She wanted peace. She didn't want to have to do treatments, in hopes that she would get pregnant again. She felt empty and didn't know if her desire to be a mother would ever happen now. Hannah didn't know if the love of her own mother, her father or the love of her husband would ever fill that space. She sat back on the bench weeping.

Soon, Aunt Melissa and her dad were standing there. Aunt Melissa sat beside her, wrapping her in her arms.

"Levi and Richard, leave us for a moment. Let me talk to Hannah," Aunt Melissa requested. Hannah remained in her aunt's arms as she had when she was a teenager.

"Sweetheart, what's going on?"

"Auntie, the doctor said I have something called endometriosis and cysts. It means we may not be able to have any kids. The doctor may have to take out my ovaries and uterus."

"That is a lot for a young married couple to hear, but you don't have to let them take your ability to have children. I know what she said, but she's not God. He can work a miracle."

Hannah continued sobbing. Attempting to wipe away her tears, she gave Aunt Melissa an unsure look.

"Auntie, why does God hate me? Why else would all this be happening to me?"

"You know God doesn't hate you. He loves you with an everlasting love. You're speaking from your pain. God loves you, Hannah. I love you. Your daddy loves you, and Levi loves you. You'll get through this. We're here. Don't consider the most extreme alternative right now. Focus on getting passed this miscarriage. I'll stay over tonight. We'll do a girls sleepover and binge watch Netflix and Lifetime movies or old episodes of *Good Times*."

Hannah gave her aunt a half smile and attempted to stand. She held her belly. There were light cramps. Aunt Melissa stood and helped her to her feet.

"Thank you, Auntie. Thank you again for always being here for me."

"It's going to be okay. We'll have a good time tonight," Aunt Melissa continued as they headed inside to find the men.

Hannah removed her cell phone from her purse and called Levi. He picked up and told her they were in the hospital cafeteria. Aunt Melissa grabbed a chair out of one of the waiting areas and instructed Hannah to sit down while she went to get the guys.

Hannah watched as her aunt turned left at the end of the main hall. She sat and waited, ready to get home and stretch out.

Moments later, Aunt Melissa, her dad and Levi returned. They were laughing at something her dad had said.

"Alright, babe. Ready to go?" Levi asked.

"Yes. I'm having a little pain."

"Well, let's get you home," Hannah's dad chimed in.

He grabbed her right arm as Levi grabbed her left and helped her to the car.

"Is Uncle Joseph still working?" Levi asked.

"Yes. He should be off in a little while. I'm going to head back home and grab some clothes to stay with you all tonight," Aunt Melissa stated.

"Thank you, Auntie," Hannah stated. "It's okay if you don't. I don't want you to have to drive home and then come back."

"I agree," Levi added.

"Oh, nonsense. That thirty-minute drive is nothing. You all need me. I'll call your uncle and let him know what's going on as well."

"How's my brother going to make it without you tonight?" Hannah's dad teased.

"He'll be alright. He'll probably grab himself something to eat and rest. He's been working some long hours lately."

"I know. So have I. I'll hang out with you and Levi a little longer, then I'll head back home."

"I understand, Daddy," Hannah stated as they helped her into the passenger seat of their car.

Although she felt numb, at that very moment, Hannah was grateful she wasn't alone. She didn't want to be left to her thoughts, not anytime soon.

***

"This is nice. Can you come over and stay more often?" Levi teased Aunt Melissa as he and Hannah entered the kitchen later that evening. Hannah agreed, taking in the sound of the fish sizzling in the deep fryer and the large spoon knocking against the small pot on their stove. Aunt Melissa was preparing one of Hannah's favorite meals, tilapia and cheese grits, the best comfort food ever. Her aunt knew how to get her to eat. She didn't know anyone who could resist Aunt Melissa's cheese grits. Hannah didn't know what her aunt couldn't cook.

The steam from the stove had caused beads of sweat to form on Aunt Melissa's forehead. She grabbed a napkin from the counter next to the refrigerator and wiped her brow.

"I would love to, but you two are married now. You need to have your own space."

"Yeah, that's true, but maybe we can build you and Uncle Joseph a room out back. It won't be that big. Just a thought," Levi said.

"You are so crazy. You and Hannah know we're not far away whenever you need either of us," Aunt Melissa reiterated, swinging the kitchen towel at him. She turned and smiled at Hannah.

"Go on. Get on out of here so I can finish cooking," Aunt Melissa ordered, laughing. Her eyes were full of joy.

"Okay," Levi said, picking up his cell phone. "I'm headed upstairs to entertain myself for the rest of the evening with a few hours of football. You ladies have fun. Auntie, please let me know when the food is ready."

"Okay, but don't you want to hang out with us girls down here?" Aunt Melissa asked.

"Ah, I'm good, Auntie. I'll survive until I fall off to sleep. I have work in the A.M."

"I understand, son. Okay then. But you're going to regret not watching these chick flicks with us on Netflix. We might even get brave enough to watch a scary movie."

"*Ummm*, I doubt it. Love you two," Levi finally said before kissing Hannah and exiting the kitchen.

Hannah stood to head into the living room. "Auntie, I'm going to watch some T.V."

"Okay, baby. Do you need anything?"

"No, I'm good," Hannah said, walking over to the couch and stretching out. She stared at the T.V. screen over their stone fireplace. Hannah got comfortable, covering herself with her favorite teal-and-brown oversized throw. She wasn't really paying attention to the show. Her mind was bombarded with their loss and the news from the doctor. She pretended to engage with a few chuckles. Her phone vibrated on the coffee table. She leaned over to see who was texting her. Her friend Robin was checking to see how she was doing. Hannah explained briefly what the doctor had shared then returned her phone to the table, not up to talking.

Aunt Melissa called into the living room a few minutes later. "You okay, sweetie? Did you already talk to your administrator for them to get you a substitute?"

"Yes," Hannah said softly.

"Okay. I'm just about done in here. The last thing I have to do is finish frying the last few pieces of this fish, and we can get this party started."

"Okay," Hannah replied, picking up her phone, scrolling through her Instagram feed. A few moments later, she sighed, waiting for Aunt Melissa to finish, needing to keep her mind occupied. She rose and headed back into the kitchen, walked over to the refrigerator for a Powerade. She sat on a stool at the island and tried to make small talk, asking Aunt Melissa how she could help. Aunt Melissa stood at the stove humming an old hymn.

"I got it, sweetie. How are you really feeling though? I noticed you seemed to be in your own world in there."

"What do you mean?"

"Remember, in order for you to heal, you have to talk through your pain. I'm here for you."

"I know you are," Hannah said just above a whisper. "I told you. I don't know what to feel, Auntie. Now, this news today," Hannah said, placing her half-finished Powerade back in the refrigerator and walking out of the kitchen. Having taken pain reliever earlier, she felt much better, so she went back to the couch and put on her slippers. Already dressed in yoga pants and a t-shirt, Hannah headed for the front door.

"Where are you going?" Aunt Melissa asked, following Hannah from the kitchen.

"For a walk, Auntie. I need some fresh air," she announced.

"You should be taking it easy, dear."

"I'll be fine. I'll be back in a few minutes."

"Okay, be safe. Make sure your phone is on you," Aunt Melissa said, her tone nervous.

"Auntie, I have it. I'm not a baby. I'll be fine," Hannah responded with frustration before closing the door.

The night breeze was welcoming as Hannah headed down the driveway. She began to cry as she walked down their brightly lit private street. Although she felt safe as she walked, Hannah's heart ached. She had looked forward to her life turning out better than her younger years. She thought back on the days when her dad struggled to keep a roof over their heads. Hannah attempted to wipe away another fountain of tears as she thought about the words of wisdom that often came from her aunt Melissa and her hairdresser, Ms. Priscilla. She made a mental note to make an appointment for next week as she ran her fingers through her hair. At the moment, she could care less what she looked like.

"God, why did you allow so much to happen to me. Ms. Priscilla and Aunt Melissa are always talking about how good you are. I don't mean to be disrespectful, but what's so bad about me? What did I do so wrong? Why does Mama seem to despise me? I need her. And why did my baby have to die? And now this endometriosis. I want to be a mother. I wanted to give our child the love I never got from Mama. I just don't get it. Can you hear me?"

Hannah stopped at the end of the block weeping. She didn't want to cry anymore but couldn't stop the tears. She wanted to move forward as she often did, but how could she? As the flow of the tears came to an end, Hannah thought she heard a soft whisper. "I'm with you. I know the thoughts I think toward you." She looked around, sure that second part was from the Bible. There was no one else on the street. It was the same voice she had heard off and on throughout the years, even as a teenager. Hannah was sure it was God speaking, but she became angered by the words, not believing, at the moment, God had any good thoughts toward her. As the words rang over and over in her ears, she ignored them and turned to head back toward home, finally realizing she had walked about two blocks.

As Hannah continued up the street, her cell phone rang. It was Robin. Hannah picked up on the second ring.

"Hello!"

"Hey, girlie. How are you doing?"

"I'm good."

"Are you sure?"

"Yes, I guess."

"How are you?"

"I'm good, but I called to check on you. I know this is hard for you, Hannah. I know you've shared things about your past with me, and it seems like your world is constantly falling apart. I can't say I understand because I've never had a miscarriage, let alone been told I possibly couldn't have any more children. I just want you to know I'm here for you. Do you want to hang out tomorrow?"

"Thanks, girl. My aunt Melissa is at the house with me. I assume she'll be with me part of tomorrow. I'll probably just stay at home and chill out. Plus, I have to take it easy for a few more days."

"Well, I can come over and keep you company if you need me to."

"No, I'll be fine."

"Okay. Call me if you need me."

"I will," Hannah finally said, disconnecting the call. As she got closer to their house, she saw a car driving in her direction. The headlights were blinding. It was their car. Levi and Aunt Melissa had come looking for her. Hannah shook her head and sighed. "I just needed a moment to myself?"

Levi pulled over to the side to allow her to climb in the front seat. Aunt Melissa sat in the back looking worried.

"Hannah, are you okay, sweetheart?"

"I'm fine, Levi. I just needed some fresh air."

"You know you should be inside."

"I just told you, I needed some fresh air, and I wanted some time to myself."

"Sweetheart, you have to talk about what you're feeling right now. Remember what the doctor said."

"Levi, I know what the doctor said. I heard her. I heard her say I probably can't have any more children! I heard her!" Hannah stated, her voice elevating. Aunt Melissa placed her hand on her shoulder from the backseat to calm her. She pulled away and turned to look out the window as they headed back home.

They pulled into their driveway and climbed out. Silence filled the air. Hannah could feel her anger rising even more. Levi opened the door and allowed Hannah and Aunt Melissa to pass. Aunt Melissa walked over to him. "Son, let me talk to her."

"You sure, Auntie?"

"I'm sure. I can handle it."

Hannah slipped out of her shoes and walked over to place her coat back into the closet then headed back to reclaim her spot on the couch. She watched as Levi opened the blinds on the sliding glass door and stepped outside. Aunt Melissa then walked toward her. Hannah clicked on the T.V. and stared at the screen.

Aunt Melissa went to the other end of the sectional. She slipped out of her shoes and moved closer to Hannah, grabbing the remote from her hand, clicking the off button. Hannah turned to look at her aunt.

"Now, I figured the miscarriage would be difficult for you, but I wasn't expecting you to receive the news about the endometriosis."

"Okay," Hannah muttered.

"Hannah, I know I came over to hang out with you, but we need to have a real conversation."

"About what, Auntie?"

"About you, sweetheart."

"What about me?" Hannah asked, sighing.

"If you don't talk about what you're feeling, especially your feelings about possibly not being able to bare children, it will cause you to push away from those of us who love you. It's normal for a woman in your situation—just losing a baby and the current revelation from the doctor—to be upset. That's part of the grieving process. Did you notice how you responded to your husband? You two are in this together."

"I'll be fine. We'll be fine. I survived all the other stuff in my life. This is just one more hurdle," Hannah stated, staring at the blank television screen.

"Yes, you'll be fine over time, but you have to go through the process of healing."

"Auntie, how do you know that?"

"Sweetheart, the loss of a baby is hard. But with God, you will heal in time."

"Maybe hurt, is just my lot in life. Kind of like what you once told me. Some people have a hard life that they can't control. I guess God is punishing me. Maybe some of the choices I made as a teenager are coming back to haunt me."

"That isn't how God operates. He loves us even while we're in our sin. Your choices were a result of your abuse. I know the beautiful person you are."

"But why then, Auntie?" Hannah asked, bawling now.

"I don't know why certain things happen. I know we live in a fallen world. Things happen to us that we can't explain. In our Bible study, we're studying about God's love. He loves each and every one of us, dear."

"Maybe God doesn't want me, like Mama."

"God isn't like people. He loves you with a love that can't be explained by man. There's nothing you can do about it. I know for sure."

"How do you know?"

"Your uncle Joseph and I were never able to have any children. I never told you this, but I had several miscarriages."

Hannah's eyes widened. She couldn't believe her aunt's revelation. She wondered how she was able to get through not one but several miscarriages. *That had to be hard.*

"Why didn't you tell me that?"

"That's not something you just start talking about, even with your loved ones."

"That's true. How'd you get through it?"

"I cried off and on for years. I thought the same way you're thinking right now. I wondered if God was punishing me. Then God sent you into my life through your dad," Aunt Melissa shared, blinking back tears.

Hannah leaned over and hugged her. They shed tears together. Hannah was grateful for her aunt. She had spent lots of time with her while her dad worked. Aunt Melissa had taught her how to cook, clean and so many other things.

After separating from each other's embrace, Hannah spoke.

"Auntie, you would have made an amazing mother. If you don't mind me asking, how many miscarriages did you have?

"Four."

"Wow. How did Uncle Joseph take it after so many tries?"

"He's been a great husband. He told me he loved me despite not being able to carry a baby to term."

"That's great. I pray Levi isn't angry with me."

"Why would he be angry? He knows it's not your fault."

"I hope so. He's a great husband too. I hope we can get through this."

"You will—with God's help."

Hannah shrugged, "I guess so."

"With time and God's healing, you will."

"By the way, did you ever find out why?" Hannah asked.

"Something about having an abnormal uterus."

"Wow."

"Yeah, but again, God brought you into my life. You've been the daughter I never had."

"Thank you for being there, Auntie."

"You know I'll be, as long as the good Lord gives me breath."

Hannah watched as her aunt closed her eyes. She knew Aunt Melissa was probably praying for her. Over the years, she had felt her many prayers. Hannah hoped to gain the strength to pray for herself and also have faith to believe as she had been taught by the amazing woman sitting right next to her, who was never forced to accept and love her. Yet, she did love her. Unconditionally.

CHAPTER SEVEN

Monday, August 31

After the most trying two weeks of her life, Hannah returned to her classroom. She winced at the pain from the menstrual cramps she once again had to endure. Her cycle was back with a vengeance. Hannah had her large bottle of Midol in her purse. She had taken two earlier. Now, she hoped the pain would go away so she could make it through the day. While at home, she'd begun researching the different endometriosis treatments to make her feel better. She had called to make an appointment with a few of the infertility specialists on the list Dr. Sarin's receptionist had given her. They were all booked for weeks. She went ahead and schedule an appointment at Dr. Calhoun's office. Hannah only chose her because she was a woman, which made her more comfortable. She couldn't get in until October.

In the meantime, Hannah planned to become more knowledgeable of the condition and the treatments. So far, she was reading about progestogens, a treatment that was supposed to relieve the symptoms by suppressing the endometriosis growth. She was considering trying it but wanted to do more research first.

Hannah had a Zoom call with her brother, Malik, on Saturday. He was checking up on her. She found herself crying as she sat talking to him. He was a man now, and she was so proud of him. Hannah told him not to worry about her. She would be fine, but the truth was, she was scared. There was no cure for endometriosis, and some of the side effects she had read for some of the treatments were not really encouraging. She felt she was too young to be trying to make these kinds of decisions that could affect her future.

Hannah was excited to see her students. She minimized her email on her computer and stood. She smiled as she stepped to the front of the room to prepare to take her students to music.

"Okay, boys and girls, let's go ahead and line up for specials."

"Ah, man! I wasn't done with my addition puzzle sheet, Mrs. Jefferson," Lesley Reynolds stated with a pout. She was probably one of the most dramatic of Hannah's third graders. *Gotta love her.*

"It's okay, Lesley. You'll have time to finish when you return," Hannah stated as she hurried the rest of the kids along.

"Yayyyy!" Lesley replied with joy after leaping to her feet and running to her cubby to grab her points sheet for music class.

"Alright, alright! Let's go, missy! We're going to have to help you stay focused to finish your work on time," Hannah stated, eyeing Leslie. "Class, go ahead and line up in the hallway."

The students filed outside like young soldiers. Hannah smiled as she grabbed her keys from the hook by the door and stepped into the hall to join them. They stood nicely in line as she turned to lock the classroom door. She had promised them a big treat the day before having to be out of her classroom. Hannah asked Robin to pass along the message, instructing them to be on their best behavior. She turned and asked Jeremiah to move the line forward. As she led her students down the hall to the music room, Hannah waved and smiled at her coworker, Anton, as he stood in his doorway awaiting the students. Her class filed inside. He waved her over, but she told him she needed to get back to her room to start grading the stack of papers on her desk.

I really don't feel like talking.

Hannah enjoyed working at Rock Lake Elementary, one of the top elementary schools in Georgia. Rock Lake had received a distinguished school award five years in a row. The students were her favorite part of her job. She felt like she was making a difference and contributing to the community.

After returning to her classroom, Hannah breathed a sigh of relief as she was able to have a quiet moment to herself. She sat at her desk, organizing her papers. Suddenly, a wave of sadness overtook her. She couldn't help but to think about the doctor's report again. Then, she began to think about the other side of her family.

She thought about the big blowup two years ago, just before she and Levi's wedding. She thought they had made amends after years of anger and resentment between them, but it was short lived after Aunt Loretta called and told her she wouldn't be attending her wedding if her husband wasn't invited. That's when Hannah had lost it. She had told her aunt not to show up because it was her special day, and it would not be ruined. She had no intentions on letting Uncle Malcolm, her molester, into the ceremony. That broke Hannah's heart, especially after her mom didn't show up either.

Brittany and Malik would sneak and call her when they were younger. Her mom would get angry with them if she found out. Hannah just didn't get why her mom seemed to despise her and her dad's side of the family. She felt there was more to her mom's anger toward them as she was reminded of her dad avoiding some of her questions over the years. Hannah planned to drill him again, and she wanted the opportunity to have a heart-to-heart with her mother. She hoped that reconciliation would be soon.

The vibration of her phone brought Hannah's attention back to the present. It was Brittany checking on her. She sent her a quick text then tried to focus to finish cleaning off her desk. It was a complete disaster. She had papers to grade and parent letters to send out.

Man, I have tons of stuff to do to catch up.

After wiping down and organizing her desk a little, Hannah began to grade the first stack of papers, a reading comprehension test from two Fridays ago. She cheered after grading Lesley's. They were all correct.

"Wow," Hannah said softly. According to Lesley's previous teacher, she came to Rock Lake last year struggling in reading and writing. "That's my girl! Now, if I can get her to improve even more academically and in her behavior this year," Hannah said to herself, making a mental note to give Lesley a treat. She looked up at the apple clock on the wall above the classroom library, realizing she only had twenty minutes remaining before having to pick up her students. Time seemed to fly when she needed to get some things done.

"Hey, girl. What's going on? Welcome back! How are you feeling?"

"Oh... Girl, you almost made me jump out of my skin. I'm good," Hannah said as she stood and walked toward the classroom door to give Robin a big hug.

"You look better than you sounded the other night. You had me worried about you," Robin stated, stepping back to size Hannah up.

"Girl, the diagnosis is just hard to believe. Being back is helping a little, helping me to focus on something else."

"That's good to hear. I came by to check on you and to ask you if you had a copy of that math lesson on double-digit subtraction you taught as a review at the beginning of the year. You said your kids seemed to get it."

"Sure. You're in luck. I just attempted to clean off my desk," Hannah stated, walking over to find the resource for her friend. "Oh, here it is."

"Thanks so much, sis."

"Not a problem at all."

"Hey, let's plan to hang out again this weekend to take your mind off everything."

"Sorry. Levi and I plan to grab some food and hang out a bit at Mama Jefferson's."

"Okay, no problem. Michael has another training. He said they're trying to prepare him to move to the next level of management."

"Oh, that's awesome."

"Yeah, I'm excited for him. I guess Community Federal Bank isn't so bad after all."

"Truth," Hannah replied.

"Alright, well I'm going to head back to my room for a few minutes. You know our planning is only five minutes."

"Five? Don't you mean three?" Hannah stated, smiling.

"That's what it feels like."

"Yep."

"Alright, girly. I'll check on you later."

"Okay. Talk to you soon."

After Robin left, Hannah walked back to her desk, wanting to finish grading the stack of papers. Then, she remembered she needed to call and pay a bill, so she grabbed her cell phone out of her purse and dialed the number to pay their utilities. Realizing she didn't have much time for anything else, Hannah put away the books that were scattered across the piece of red carpet in front of the bookshelf. She then went over to the sink to clean it. Once she was done, it was time to pick up her students. Hannah headed back down to the music room.

Dang, I didn't get anything done.

As she got closer, she noticed Anton already had her students lined up in the hallway as usual. Abigail was whispering to Shanna in front of her. She stopped when she noticed her walking toward them. Hannah shook her head and smiled.

My little Abigail.

She walked past the line and stepped inside the music room where Anton was standing just inside the door talking to Lesley who had tears in her eyes.

"What's going on, Mr. Jones?" Hannah asked, curious.

"Lesley, do you want to tell Mrs. Jefferson?"

Lesley shook her head and started crying even more.

I am so not in the mood for this nonsense today.

"Okay, go ahead and join your classmates in line outside."

"Okay!" Lesley said softly with tears streaming down her face.

"Okay, what's up?" Hannah asked.

"Lesley called Jeremiah an ugly, stupid boy when she couldn't get to the drums because he was already there," Anton informed Hannah, trying to keep a straight face.

Hannah chuckled. "I'm so sorry. I shouldn't be laughing."

"So, I told her that she wouldn't get any points for today, and she's all upset now. Lord, help!"

"Okay, thanks, Anton. I'll have a long talk with her when we get back to the room. Hopefully, we won't have this issue again, or I'm going to have to call for a parent conference. I love her. She's the sweetest little girl, but I've seen several of these tantrums already, and it's just August."

"She may be a little spoiled," Anton added.

"Yeah, I didn't think of that. Okay, see you next week." *So is your daughter,* Hannah thought, not daring to say that out loud.

"By the way, how are you doing? I noticed you'd been out," he said before Hannah could walk away.

"I'm okay."

"That's good. Is everything okay?"

Dang, nosey, Hannah thought, looking out the window at her students. She stared for a moment before turning back toward him.

"Yes, I'm good."

"Well, if you need anything, let me know."

No, I'm good, Hannah thought. "Okay, thanks," she finally said out loud and headed for the door. She exited the room and stepped into the hallway where her students were still standing like soldiers. She had seen some talking through the window, but they had stopped when they saw her.

"Alright, boys and girls, let's head back to class. We have math and social studies, then you'll be headed home in a little bit."

As the students marched back down the hall. Principal Hall happened to be coming out of his office.

"Wow, awesome line, Mrs. Jefferson. And welcome back."

"Thank you, Mr. Hall." Hannah could hear the kids cheering quietly. They loved compliments. They knew they were closer to their treat or extra recess time, but she hadn't decided. After stopping by the restroom, the class finally made it back to the room and headed back to their seats. Lesley was still crying softly. Hannah loved her job. She just had to wear so many hats. As the other students got settled, Hannah called Lesley over to her desk for a quick chat. She tried to encourage her but also made her aware that her behavior was unacceptable. Lesley finally calmed down and returned to her desk to get ready for math.

"Okay, ladies and gents, if you haven't already, take out your math workbooks."

"Yes, ma'am," a few of them said. Others groaned.

Hannah did an opening word problem after pulling up Active Inspire that gave her the ability to write on the worksheet she had also pulled up. Some of the students were excited to come up and write on it using what they called the magic pen. She looked around to see who else she could call and noticed lots of confused looks, so she worked out a few more problems slowly, instructing them to practice step by step with her on their paper.

Next, she assigned more problems to the class. She then headed to the back table to work with the group that was still struggling while some of the other students practiced at the board and others at their seats. Hannah smiled when Harold got the hang of it. He then wanted to teach the others in the group, so Hannah allowed it and guided him. He started with Lesley. She was reluctant at first, but then got excited when she got the hang of it. Hannah winked at her and smiled.

"See, I got it, Mrs. Jefferson. I even taught them," Harold said with excitement.

"Okay, so you'll also get some practice problems tonight. I want you to show your mom or dad what you've learned."

"Okay. I'll show my mom. My dad is gone a lot, and I don't see him as much."

Hannah made a mental note to talk to her students about not telling all of their parents' business. As she watched the next student practice, she thought about some of the crazy stories she had heard last year alone, then her mind drifted again to the endometriosis. She still couldn't wrap her mind around possibly not becoming a mother. She was grateful to be able to teach such awesome little people. Each year, she treated her students like her own, but they belonged to their parents, not to her.

Fifteen minutes later, Hannah called for the students to transition into social studies. She heard loud moans. Each year, she noticed how much many of her students hated social studies. She tried her best to make it fun, but some of it was so dry.

"Okay, guys and ladies, let's get our social studies lesson done before we pack up to go home. Grab your interactive notebooks."

"Yes, ma'am!" the class echoed in submission.

Hannah headed back to the front of the room and pulled up her interactive presentation on the three branches of government. She hoped the students would like this one. Jeremiah raised his hand and asked, "Mrs. Jefferson, I'm so glad you are back. I love you being my teacher, but why do we have to know all of this social studies stuff? We're just kids. Who cares about the government. I can't even vote yet."

"I agree, Jeremiah, but the state requires that you learn it at this age. It's never too early to learn about your government and the role you and others play as citizens." *He is too much. Who is he listening to at the house?* Hannah wondered.

"Okay, if you say so, Mrs. J," Jeremiah added with a look of exasperation.

"Come on, guys. This will be quick and painless."

"Okay," the class said with a drawl.

Hannah started her presentation and had the students to role-play a scenario for the different branches. Some of them started giggling and pointing as the others played the roles. Hannah noticed they were enjoying themselves. She allowed them to switch roles for about twenty minutes and then did a wrap-up by asking what they had learned. Many of the students shared all that had stuck with them. *My work here is done! They got it!* Hannah then instructed the students to get packed up. As they were gathering their things, the announcements came on.

"Good afternoon, everyone. It's time for dismissal. Here are a few announcements: Don't forget the PTO bake sale. Mr. Jones would like to meet with the music club after school on Thursday right after the bell. Okay, please dismiss your car riders," the older student sang over the intercom.

Hannah hurried her students along. The car riders dashed out the door. The bus riders talked and helped stack the chairs while they waited for their numbers to be called. After all the students had left, Hannah sat for a few minutes to finish cleaning off her desk. She then packed her bags quickly to head to the car. She was anxious to get home, get a shower and keep her mind occupied with the Lifetime movie marathon that was on this week. She also planned to get back to researching the various treatments for endometriosis, those that gave her a better chance at conceiving again. She had found a few more and had taken down several notes, but she really hoped to find a natural treatment for her condition. This day had surely helped her to take her mind off of everything she had experienced. Hannah couldn't wait until tomorrow. She had gained some strength from her students.

CHAPTER EIGHT

❖

Tuesday, September 8

After getting settled in from a long day, Hannah fluffed her pillows on her side of the bed and got comfortable. She leaned back against the pillows and clicked on the television in their bedroom. She then grabbed her cell phone from the nightstand and clicked to dial Brittany's number. Her sister picked up on the first ring.

"Hello," Brittany said, sniffling.

"Sis, what's going on? I wanted to check on you since you hadn't called in a few days."

"I don't know what to do."

"About what, Brit? You're scaring me."

"You're going to be disappointed in me."

"What's going on?"

"I found out Friday that I'm pregnant."

"What?" Hannah said, her voice elevating.

"Yes. I'm scared, Hannah. I didn't mean for this to happen. I told Travis, and he got angry."

"He did what?"

"He started telling me he doesn't have time for no babies right now and how he's getting ready to graduate."

"That was selfish of him," Hannah fumed.

"How could he do me like that, sis?"

"Brittany, it's going to be alright. I'm here for you. I'll help you as much as I can, when I can."

"It's not going to be okay," Brittany sobbed. "I'm not married yet. I can't have a baby and live on campus. Plus, I don't have any money saved up.

What's Mama going to say? Hannah, I can't go back to live with her. I'm sorry."

"Brittany, calm down. I'm here."

"Then Travis dismissed me, talking about 'have an abortion or put the baby up for adoption.'"

"That raggedy joker," Hannah spat.

"I'm so embarrassed. I refuse to have an abortion, but I can't be a single mother. And I don't want to drop out of college," Brittany ranted, now hysterical.

"Relax, Brittany. Where are you now?"

"In the dorm parking lot in my car. I have a paper due and a quiz coming up, but I can't focus."

"I want you to relax and take a deep breath. You have to do well in your classes."

"Okay," Brittany replied, sniffling.

"I love you. I'm here for you. You can come here and study if you need to."

"No. I'll try to go over to the campus library. I have to try. The paper is due by Friday."

"Okay, well call me if you need me."

"I will. Love you."

"Love you too."

Hannah sighed. She felt as if she was in a bad dream. *Am I cursed or something? My unprepared to take care of a child and unmarried sister gets pregnant, but I lose my baby and get diagnosed with endometriosis and possibly can't get pregnant again. How unfair.* As soon as the thought came and went, Hannah felt guilty for simply thinking it. She felt awful thinking about herself right now. Unable to focus, she got up and headed into the office. Hannah logged in and began researching endometriosis. Several articles came up. She grabbed a notebook from her stack on the top shelf in the closet. Her heart ached for Brittany and herself. She knew her sister needed her, but it was so hard not to think about her own situation. *Really, God? Why do I have to go through this?*

She read another article about progestogens and took down several notes. As she clicked back to the article list, Hannah noticed an ad for a free trial with ancestry.com. Having dismissed it numerous times, this time she decided to check out. Hannah clicked on it and typed in her information to set up an account. Still hoping to find out more about her family on both her mom and dad's side, Hannah abandoned her article reading and began to build her family tree. She searched the records for her grandparents on her mom's side first. Getting excited when she located information about her mom's mom, Grandma Liz, she then searched for her great-grandparents. There was more info about them. The research was a great distraction for Hannah.

Hannah found out that her great-grandfather was in the military. After adding it to the tree, she opened Grandma Liz's death certificate. She verified her great-grandparents' names, and her mom was listed as the informant. *I wonder if that means she was the person who provided this information.*

She then searched for her mom. There was limited information, but there was another death certificate listed. It was for someone named Terrance Singleton. She clicked on it. *Who is this person?* Hannah began to read the document. She froze when she saw her mom's name. *Wait, what?*

"Mama was married to this guy? Why are their last names different? This doesn't make any sense."

Hannah scanned the rest of the document and noticed the date of death. Hannah shuddered. She was one year old at the time. She closed out of the document and frantically searched for more information. She couldn't find much, but a marriage license. Hannah quickly opened it. Her hands trembled as she attempted to keep the mouse steady. She scrolled back to the top and noticed that her mom and the Terrance guy were married before she was born.

Hannah felt nauseous.

Is this real? This man couldn't have been my dad? No, Richard Monroe is my dad. Hannah stood and paced the office floor. "I've got to call Daddy. This is crazy. Why did I even click on that?"

Moments later, Hannah heard the garage door opening.

She rushed out of the office and bounded down to tell Levi what she had discovered. Now, standing at the door leading to the garage, Hannah wringed her hands. She unlocked the door and opened it. Levi looked at her and smiled.

"Why do you look so nervous? Are you okay?" Levi asked, kissing her.

"No. I was doing more research on endometriosis treatments, and I found out..." Hannah stammered.

"Found out what? Babe, what's wrong?"

"While I was researching, I came across this free trial for ancestry.com."

"What? Haven't we both seen that a thousand times? You decided to try it out today?"

"Yes. I was just curious and wanted to know more about my family."

"So, what did you find out that's got you so upset?" Levi asked, following Hannah into the kitchen. Levi put his keys in their junk drawer and took a seat at the island.

"I found out that Mama was married to some guy named Terrance Singleton."

"Huh? I thought your mama was only married to Brittany and Malik's dad before."

"I did too, but based on what I found, they were married before I was born."

"What's wrong with that?"

"You're not getting what I'm saying. They were married when I was born."

"Oh, O..." Levi said, his eyes wide.

"Right."

"Well, I'm sure there's an explanation for it."

"I hope so. And this Terrance guy died when I was one."

"How do you know that?"

"I read the death certificate. Mama signed it as the wife."

"Okay. This is too much. It's sounding like this guy could have been your dad."

"Exactly."

"Okay, okay. Naw, babe. I know what it says, but there has to be another explanation. You look just like Pops Monroe."

"That's what people have said since I was younger, and Daddy said I look just like his mom."

"Right, so we are not going to allow any doubts into our minds. Just call Pops and ask him about it."

"I plan to. Remember I told you, over the years, I've asked Daddy different questions, and he's avoided the ones about why Mama is so angry toward him and me."

"Well, it's time for him to tell you what's really going on."

"I agree. I have to admit that I'm nervous. I don't know what I would do if I found out that Daddy isn't my real dad."

"You know that isn't true. Call and talk to him," Levi encouraged.

"Okay. I'll fix us something to eat and then give Daddy a call," Hannah stated.

"Sounds good."

"Oh, yeah. I forgot."

What?" Levi asked.

"I also talked to Brittany earlier. I had to calm her down. She was hysterical," Hannah announced, pulling the ground turkey from the refrigerator and grabbing a pan from beneath the cabinet next to the stove.

"Why? What's going on with her?"

"She found out she's pregnant," Hannah said, turning to look at Levi's expression. She then pulled the seasoning salt and black pepper from the upper cabinets and sat them on the counter as she turned back toward Levi.

"Nooooo," Levi said, rubbing his hands over the top of his bald head.

"Yes, and she's so scared, and trifling Travis told her to get rid of it or put the baby up for adoption."

"He didn't tell her that."

"Yes, he did."

"He better not let me lay eyes on him, that's all I know."

"I felt the same way, but we can't go beat him up. We would both lose our jobs."

"I can pay somebody."

"Stop playing, Levi. You know you can't do anything like that."

"Why not?"

"You can't. We just have to try to help Brittany where and when we can. She's terrified of having to drop out of school and of what Mama is going to say."

"That's a lot to think about, that's for sure."

"It is," Hannah said, finally turning back to season the ground turkey to prepare a few turkey burgers. "My heart goes out to her. She feels like she let me down. She said she feels so embarrassed."

"Yeah, babe. No disrespect, but Brittany knows all about the birds and the bees. She's also embarrassed because she knows what the Bible says about sex outside of marriage."

"Does she? I mean, I was taught the Word. You were taught the Word, but Mama wasn't the best example nor was the Word a priority, even when I lived with Mama. Daddy, Aunt Melissa, and Uncle Joseph were the ones who brought me up in the Word and were good examples in my life and look at me."

"What do you mean?" Levi asked.

"I've been struggling with my faith a little because of all of the craziness I've had to endure over the years. This was even before losing the baby. Now, I don't know what to feel."

"Seriously?" Levi asked with a surprised expression. "Is that why you don't really want to attend church?"

"Yes. Levi, I want to trust God, I really do, but I don't know how to. I feel angry with him sometimes. I feel that he's been punishing me most of my life."

"Babe, you know that isn't true."

"That's what it feels like, especially now. I mean, I want to know God like those who have taught me over the years, but I wonder if I can surrender and really put my trust in Him. Think about what I just found online."

"Hannah, just like Mama and my pops taught me from the time I was small, I'm telling you that God loves you. I've felt His presence, even when I was doing my dirt. When Pops passed, I never felt that God didn't love me. I've always felt his love. God isn't people."

"I honestly haven't felt that way a lot of the time, Levi. Maybe in my teens, but not since."

"But you just said you didn't know if you could surrender to or trust him. You've got to let your guard down."

"I guess you're right," Hannah said, turning back to finish preparing their turkey burgers.

"I know I am," Levi said, wrapping his arms around her waist and kissing her neck. Hannah's shoulders relaxed at his touch.

"Let's try to be there for Brit. We know Mama is going to tear her down. We have to love her through this," Hannah said.

"I agree. God would want us to love her."

"Thanks, Hannah said, pulling out the large frying pan as Levi walked to the entrance of the kitchen.

"You don't have to thank me."

"I know, but I'm grateful to have you."

"I'm grateful for you too. And just remember, you can't fix what you're experiencing or have experienced. Neither can you fix your family. Only God can, and he will never treat you like people."

"I miss these talks. We're always so busy, running in and out to and from work," Hannah said, turning to face him again.

"I miss this too. I want you to know that I love you regardless. You know Mama has always been able to see you as my wife."

"I know. I remember the first time she told you, one of those times we visited her in college."

"Oh yeah. I ain't gon' lie. I thought Mama was tripping."

"Well, she wasn't. I'm right here," Hannah said, adding another turkey burger into the pan.

"Right. Now hurry up and finish. Yo' man is hungry."

"You are so crazy."

"Alright, I'm going to head up and take a shower."

"Okay. I should be done with these last two by the time you're done."

After Levi left the kitchen, Hannah thought about his words. She wanted to trust God. She didn't want to be angry. Now, she had to find out if she had been lied to all of these years.

How do I get passed losing the baby? The endometriosis? Everything from my past and this foolishness I just found? It hurts, Hannah said in her heart. As she finished up their quick meal, she heard, *Surrender your pain and your heart to me.* But she didn't even know how and where to start.

***

Bright and early the next morning, Hannah entered the doors of Rock Lake Elementary. She felt better, but still found herself crying on and off. She hadn't called her dad to ask about the information she'd found. She was too afraid. She was also worried about her sister, and she wanted the endometriosis diagnosis to disappear. Hannah's mind was bombarded with too much. She headed into the cafeteria to grab some cereal. Hannah spoke to two of the kindergarten paraprofessionals, Mrs. Howard and Mr. Johnson, and Assistant Principal Watson as they stood holding what looked like a heavy conversation. Hannah headed over to the table by the door, not wanting them to think she was trying to listen in. She could care less what they were talking about.

After her first year at Rock Lake, Hannah began to notice cliques forming. She loved teaching there, but she could do without the drama that was part of the package. Hannah would often tell herself, "I'm here for my babies." That's what kept her pressing forward and not reenrolling in college to start a new major.

Hannah sat and ate quickly while listening to a new audiobook by Francine Rivers. She had enjoyed the way the author unfolded the other story and kept her interest throughout. A few minutes later, Hannah tossed her container into the trashcan and headed toward the bus loading zone. *Wow, this is another amazing story,* Hannah thought as she turned down the fifth-grade hall.

"Good morning, Mrs. Jefferson," Mr. Clark, a fifth-grade teacher, said cheerfully.

"Good morning," Hannah replied, not slowing her pace.

She walked out and stood waiting for the first set of buses to pull in. This was her second year being selected for bus duty. She and Ms. Hawkins, a second-grade teacher, were given the joy of greeting the students first thing in the morning. Ms. Hawkins seemed to always have an excuse as to why she couldn't be on bus duty, or she was late coming in most mornings. Mr. Hall would also come out to greet the students with her, but he had a principal's meeting this morning. Hannah was grateful for the few moments of tranquility. A few minutes later, the lion bus pulled in. The students had been so confused with the number system that the transportation manager changed it to names of animals. The older students thought it was too babyish, but after so many of them lost their bus numbers and agendas, the change was made to save time on having to pick up and drop off the high school students on time. They didn't have a huge district, so the bus drivers had to complete more than one route.

The bus driver, Mrs. Stockman, opened the doors, and the students bounded off. Hannah waved at her as she seemed to be listening to instructions from dispatch. She smiled and waved back.

"Good morning," Hannah sang to the students.

"Good morning," some grumbled with sleep still in their eyes. She smiled and continued to usher them toward the cafeteria.

"Good morning, Isabelle and Allen." Hannah hugged a few of her students from last year. "How's class going? Are you behaving?"

"Yes, ma'am," Isabelle stated. "Not Allen though. He talks back to Mrs. Springer."

"I do not, Stop lying." Allen looked at Isabella with anger.

"Okay, guys. Go on in and behave. Make me proud."

"Yes, ma'am," they both said as Allen kept his eye on Isabelle.

Hannah remembered seeing some of that anger in Allen last year. She would give him recess detention at least once a week. He would improve for a time, then he was right back to his old ways. Hannah remembered mentioning her concerns to Allen's mother.

She was nonchalant and stated, "Well, his daddy ain't here half of the time, so he starts showing his behind. I don't have time to keep talking to that boy and coming to that school. I have to work. If I lose my job, then what?"

Hannah often felt helpless when she heard some of her students' situations. She wondered why some people were able to have children, but she was being punished. A few moments later, two more buses pulled in. The students hurried off and ran toward the cafeteria. The bell would be ringing in ten minutes. Hannah shouted her hellos and hugged a few more as she stood on the sidewalk in their pathway. She then turned and noticed the last six buses pulling in.

She dashed quickly toward her classroom with two minutes to spare before her students would be sent down from the gym. She only had time to turn on the lights, her computer and the student computers.

I've got to start getting here a little earlier, so I have everything set up before my morning duty, Hannah reminded herself.

When she started three years ago, she would come in at least thirty minutes early to set up. Then, it seemed the demands increased, so Hannah would make it in just in time to complete her required responsibilities. She knew she had to do better, no matter what.

Later that morning, Hannah was in the middle of trying to get her third graders to understand the difference between main idea and theme when she noticed Mrs. Henderson, the school clerk, at the door with a student and her family. She was a new student, a beautiful African-American girl, who could have been related to her. She wore pigtails and had a deep bronze complexion. Her yellow dress and the yellow barrettes she wore highlighted her complexion even more. Hannah noticed the terrified look on the girl's face as she neared the doorway where they all stood. Suddenly, Hannah froze as she stared into the little girl's eyes. She blinked back tears wondering if that was what her child would have looked like. She couldn't pull her eyes away.

"*Ummm,* are you okay, Mrs. Jefferson?" Mrs. Henderson asked.

"*Ummm,* yes," Hannah managed to say, stepping into the hallway.

"Well, good morning. Sorry to interrupt. This is Amani Newman, a new student," Mrs. Henderson stated, handing Hannah a copy of the student's registration. Hannah also noticed her transportation information listed on the yellow sticky note on top. Mrs. Henderson then turned toward the parents. "And this is Mr. and Mrs. Newman."

"It's very nice to meet you," Mr. Newman stated, extending his hand toward Hannah.

"Same here," Hannah replied, shaking both of their hands. "I'm Mrs. Jefferson. Nice to meet you. I'm excited to have Amani. I'll be sending home some information with her this afternoon."

"Okay. We're going to head back up front," Mrs. Henderson replied as Hannah turned back toward Amani.

"Let's go on in, sweetie."

Hannah ushered the young lady in to an empty desk as Mrs. Henderson walked her parents back toward the front lobby. Hannah then introduced Amani to the rest of the class.

"Class, let's welcome our new student, Amani Newman." Hannah felt Amani move closer to her.

"Hello," the students said in unison.

"Can she sit next to me, Mrs. Jefferson?" Lesley asked with excitement.

"No. She can take this empty seat next to Harold."

"Ah, man," Lesley blurted out. "I want her to be next to me."

"Lesley, it's okay. You can get to know Amani more at recess."

"Okay," Lesley said with her bottom lip pushed out for effect.

"Okay, ladies and gentlemen, let's get back to our reading instruction. "Amani, we're getting ready to read *Ms. Nelson is Missing*. Afterward, we'll write about the main idea and the theme of the story. You all will share with the class." Amani didn't respond. She just sat with her hands in her lap, wringing them together nervously. "Are you okay, sweetheart?" Hannah asked. Amani looked up at her and nodded.

Hannah started the story; the other students were eager to hear. The cover made them curious. As she read, she couldn't help but think about Amani. She hoped she would loosen up soon. Hannah wondered if she should have allowed her to sit next to Lesley, her little chatty Kathy.

As she got toward the middle of the story, the students were all engaged. Hannah could hear a pin drop. As she scanned the room, she once again began to picture what her child would have looked like. Hannah shook her head and began to blink back more tears.

"Are you okay, Mrs. Jefferson?" Harold asked, bringing Hannah's mind back to what she was doing.

"Ah, yes. How about you talk to your partner next to you about what you have learned so far about the story."

Hannah then walked over to her desk. With her back turned to the class, she wiped away her tears with the tissue she retrieved from her desk. She attempted to gather herself so she could make it through the day. The next thing she knew, there was a tap on her arm.

"Ah, Mrs. Jefferson, are you sure you're okay? You look sad," Abigail stated, looking up at her with those beautiful round eyes and curly blond hair.

"Yes, sweetie. I'm fine. Now, go on over to your seat and finish discussing the story."

"Okay," Abigail replied with concern.

Okay, Hannah. Get your life together. You can't be breaking down in front of the kids.

After taking another minute to gather herself, Hannah returned to the front of the room. She asked a few questions. The students almost fought over who would answer. She smiled and soon began reading the story again. The students were enjoying it. She looked over at Amani. She still looked nervous, but Hannah noticed a slight smile on her face this time. She wasn't sure why she was drawn to the child. *Okay, keep going.* Hannah continued reading and finished a few minutes later. Hands shot up with more questions and comments.

"Now, I have some questions for you to answer on the board. You're going to work with a partner to answer them in your composition notebook, then you'll turn to your partner on the left or right and share your thoughts. After that, we'll discuss as a group."

"Okayyyyyy," said some of the students, eager to speak.

As the students were writing, Hannah looked around, making sure everyone was on task and checking to see if anyone needed her assistance. She then walked over to her desk to sit down, something she had been doing more often. As she sat, she asked how many were still working. A few hands raised. Hannah waited a few more minutes.

When most students were done, Hannah called on Tessa to go first. As always, Lesley got upset. *This li'l girl. Way too old to be throwing tantrums.* As Tessa stood and began reading, Hannah went and stood next to Lesley. When she started tapping her pencil on the desk out of frustration, Hannah placed her hand on Lesley's shoulder to get her attention. She stopped, and the class was able to hear Tessa. She was very intelligent but was reluctant to speak in front of the class. After Tessa, Hannah allowed Lesley to share. She noticed that her main idea was not quite on target but allowed her to continue because she knew what the response would be if she gave her any feedback now. She would pull Lesley while the others practiced math skills; Lesley was better at math.

A few more students shared, then Hannah began to write and explain on the board. The students started noticing where they got confused. After wrapping up the reading lesson, Hannah breathed a sigh of relief as she told the kids to get ready for P.E., and she headed back to her desk.

Why can't I stop thinking about it? We could still keep trying.

"Are you okay, Mrs. Jefferson?" Lesley now asked, patting Hannah on the arm.

"Oh, yeah. I'm fine."

"You sure?"

"I'm fine, missy. Now, go get ready for P.E." *Man, my students are nosier than some grown-ups.*

"Do I have to? Can I stay with you?"

"No, you have to go to P.E., missy."

"*Awww,* man," Lesley said, stomping her feet and walking away. Hannah shook her head. She was surely a handful. A few minutes later, Hannah lined up the class. She marched them down to the other end of the building where the gym was located. She waved at Coach Wright as he headed out of his office on the other side to receive the students.

"It's good to see you," he said.

"Thanks," Hannah replied.

"Alright, boys and girls, take a seat on the mat," Coach Wright instructed as Hannah closed the gym door. She hurried to make her way back to her classroom to continue working on the mounds of paperwork on her desk. As she passed the music room, she found herself wiping away more tears. She thought returning to work would help, but her mind was bombarded with her life. She turned on the back hall by the art room. There were very few classrooms there, and she could avoid as many people as possible.

Once she got to her hall, she peeked in the window of Robin's classroom. Robin was sitting over in the corner near her desk in the back of the room. Hannah stepped inside, announcing herself.

"Hey, girlie."

"Oh, what's going on?" Robin asked, standing and walking toward Hannah. "You decided to skip the paperwork and stop by and hang out for five minutes?"

"Yes. What are you up to?" Hannah asked, looking around her friend at the papers scattered on the floor in stacks.

"Girl, I'm trying to sort my students' papers to file in their folders and send home on Friday."

"*Oooh,* I guess I need to do that too."

"Yep! So, what's up?" Robin asked, eyeing Hannah.

"Nothing much."

"Yes, it is. Spill it."

"I didn't get a chance to tell you what I found yesterday."

"What?"

Hannah explained to Robin the information she stumbled on about the man her mom was once married to, the fear of confronting her dad and finding out even more bad news, and the news about her sister. Her eyes filled with tears, wanting the hurricane that her life had been for years to return to a tropical storm. Without asking permission, Robin grabbed her hands and begin to pray. When Robin was done, Hannah stood to grab a tissue from the corner of her desk. Feeling better, Hannah hugged her friend and chatted with her for a bit. Somehow, she believed that Robin would become an even greater support in her life, greater than she had already been.

CHAPTER NINE

Friday, September 18

After trying to get up enough nerve to call and ask her dad about her findings on ancestry.com, her sister's depressed state about her pregnancy, reading more depressing articles about endometriosis with so many side effects, and feeling as if she were on an emotional roller coaster after her miscarriage, Hannah was glad to still be at work. She needed the distraction. Her desire to be a mother and wanting to build a relationship with her own mother consumed her. She was exhausted.

Hannah sat at her kidney table with her co-worker and former classmate, Anton, and her student Lesley's mom. Lesley had been acting out more and more, and they were finally able to get her mom in for a conference. Hannah had called her mom on Tuesday after her tantrum in the cafeteria. Then, on Wednesday, she stomped on Amani's foot, accusing her of taking her new pencil. Hannah scolded Lesley. She then began to dump everything out of her desk. Hannah called for her to be removed until she calmed down. Mrs. Watson, her assistant principal, instructed her to contact the parent for a conference after taking her students to specials.

It was now after school hours on a Friday. Even though this conference was a much-needed distraction, Hannah was not in the mood for Lesley's mom's attitude. She listened as Anton explained what he had observed in music for the past few weeks.

"Mrs. Reynolds, as I stated, Lesley is a great kid. We want what's best for her. That's why I wanted to be in this conference with Mrs. Jefferson."

"Don't you think I want what's best for my child? You sit here and tell me about her behaviors. Isn't that what normal children do? They get mad. They throw tantrums."

"No, Mrs. Reynolds, some of the behaviors Lesley is displaying are not normal," Hannah interjected.

"Excuse me, but do you have any children, Mrs. Jefferson?"

"No, I don't, but we aren't talking about me. We're discussing Lesley right now," Hannah retorted.

"Well, you and Mr. Jones here obviously don't know what it's like being a parent."

"*Ummm,* Mrs. Reynolds, I have a daughter in the fifth grade, so I'm well aware," Anton stated.

"Well, I have four children I'm trying to take care of by myself. My husband walked out on us three years ago, and I've been trying to keep a roof over our heads. I should be at work right now, not sitting here in this meaningless meeting with you two. And Lesley told me you seem to like that other little girl more than her. She said the little girl took her pencil, and she got upset. She said she tried to apologize, but you yelled at her," said Mrs. Reynold's eyeing Hannah.

"Mrs. Reynold's, the other student had the same pencil. She and Lesley showed them to me the other day. And Lesley did not try to apologize."

"Are you calling my daughter a liar?"

"I did not say that. I'm only sharing with you what I observed."

"I don't have time for this. Is this conference over?" asked Lesley's mom.

"We are almost done," Anton interjected, trying to sound cheerful. Hannah was tired of this craziness. She couldn't hold back her question.

"Excuse me, but isn't Lesley's well-being more important to you?" Hannah asked with irritation. She thought back to the short time she had lived with her mom. This woman reminded her of her mom. She never seemed concerned about anything else except those men in her life, drinking, and how her bills were going to be paid. Anton eyed Hannah, seeming to try to get her to calm down.

"Excuse me, you sit up in here with your little degree and talk to me about my child's well-being. How old are you? How dare you? Who do you think you are? You're no better than me."

"I didn't say anything like that. I only a—"

"Well, worry about your own children. Oh, that's right, you don't have any," Mrs. Reynolds spewed.

Hannah felt as though she had just been punched in the gut. She couldn't believe it. *The audacity of this parent.*

"Mrs. Reynolds, you know nothing about my situation, so I would rather we keep the conversation about your child," Hannah stated, a little louder than she intended to.

"Who are you raising your voice at?"

"I didn't mean to raise my voice, Mrs. Reynolds. I was simply asking that we keep this about your daughter and not me. As we were trying to explain, Lesley has been acting out. How can you work with us to assist your daughter? I want the principal's office to be the last resort."

"How about I contact your principal's office in the morning about your little attitude?"

"I don't have an attitude, Mrs. Reynolds. I simply asked how you can assist us at home. Lesley is your child, not mine. We need your assistance," Hannah spat. Anton eyed her again. *This lady is about to make me lose it up in here.*

"Well, being that I'm at work until late in the evening and my older daughter helps me with the younger kids, I would have to see what I can do to help correct Lesley's behavior."

"Is your older daughter helping Lesley with her homework as well?"

"Yes. Do you have an issue with that? I have to work."

"Are you able to sit with her at any point during the week?"

"When I get a chance, Mrs. Jefferson! What is your issue?"

I have an issue with you not wanting to help your daughter. But I'm the one being punished. I'm the one who lost my child and may not be able to have more. You sit up in here and act like your child is not a priority to you, Hannah fumed, knowing she would possibly lose her job if she said what she was thinking.

"*Ummm,* Mrs. Jefferson, let me talk to Mrs. Reynolds," Anton said, as if he were about to referee a fight.

"No problem," Hannah said, trying to keep her composure. She stood, grabbed her phone, and walked out of the room. She walked toward the teacher's workroom on their hall. *Why would she say such things? She doesn't even know me. How can she be someone's parent—more concerned about herself? Those children need her. Just like I needed Mama.*

Hannah stepped into the workroom and grabbed a chair. She sat at the table in the middle of the room. She wasn't sure if she was angrier with Lesley's mom because she sounded much like hers or about the *being a parent* comment she had made without any thought of her as a person. Soon, tears streamed down her cheeks. Her right leg shook because she wanted to give

Mrs. Reynolds a piece of her mind. As she reflected on the parent's words, more tears came. Her head throbbing, Hannah lay it in the palms of her hands.

Why am I letting her words get to me? What am I going to do with Lesley because her mama is clearly no help? Hannah wondered.

As she sat for a bit longer trying to pull herself together, her phone vibrated. She opened it. It was Brittany. She hadn't called in the last few days. Hannah had texted her the other day to encourage her. She read her sister's message.

I need to talk to you, sis.

Is everything okay? Hannah replied, wiping away her tears.

Yes. I just have something important to ask you.

Okay. Well I'm still at the school right now. I can try to call you when I get in the car.

Okay, Brittany replied.

After a few more minutes, Hannah walked back to her classroom, grateful to see Mrs. Reynolds leaving. *What a waste of time.* When she entered the room, Anton was still sitting at the back table writing on the conference form they were instructed to fill out when they met with a parent.

"Were you able to get anything accomplished?"

"Not really. She's really stressed out with having to work so much."

"Who cares about her stress? She needs to be concerned with Lesley—and her other children."

"Hannah, it's hard on some parents."

"I'm aware of that. I was raised by a single parent, remember?"

"So, can you be a little more understanding?" Anton pleaded.

"I guess, but I don't appreciate those things she said to me."

"I agree. She was out of line, but we have to be sensitive too."

"Out of line? She was straight-up rude, Anton, and you know it. How was I expected to be sensitive?"

"Are you okay?"

"Yes. What do you mean?"

"Your eyes are red."

"I'm fine. I just got frustrated with that parent."

"Are you sure?"

"It's nothing," Hannah said, sitting at her desk.

"It doesn't seem like nothing," Anton said, walking closer to her.

"I told you. I'm fine."

"It seemed like something triggered in you when she talked about being a parent."

"What do you mean?"

"You looked like you wanted to claw out her eyes for a minute, and I've never seen you get that angry with anyone, even when people used to try you in college."

"Did I really look at her that way?"

"Oh, yes."

"Well, I'm good—just can't believe these parents sometimes," Hannah stated, choking back more tears.

"Some of these parents have real struggles."

"My dad had real struggles, but he didn't make excuses."

"Are you sure nothing else is wrong?"

"Nothing," Hannah replied, trying to sound convincing.

"Well, nothing might get you in the principal's office. That parent mentioned calling."

"She did?" Hannah asked with a little concern.

"Yeah. Hopefully I talked her down."

"Thanks for being here. I might have lost it."

"No problem."

"Maybe my wife and I can get together with you and Levi sometime."

"That would be cool."

"I'll check with her to see and get back with you."

"Okay," Hannah replied, hoping it was no time soon. She wasn't up to it.

"Well, let me know if you need anything."

"I will."

"It will work out."

"Huh?" Hannah asked, confused at his comment.

"Whatever it is, it will work out."

"Thanks, but I told you I'm good."

"If you say so. Alright, I'll see you."

"Okay, Thanks again," Hannah said as Anton grabbed his things and headed toward the door.

"Alright. Have a great weekend," Hannah called out to him as he exited her classroom.

"You too," he yelled.

As Hannah gathered her belongings, she thought about the anger she felt toward Mrs. Reynolds. As she headed to her car, Anton's words replayed in her mind. "You looked like you wanted to claw her eyes out."

Hannah had no idea the anger she felt showed. *But she had no right to say those rude things to me,* Hannah thought. That parent had no clue how much her words had cut. She felt as if the woman had ripped the scab off a deep gash that had not yet begun to heal.

On the way home, Hannah called to see what was up with Brittany. She didn't answer at first but called right back. Hannah didn't like how sad her sister sounded.

"Hey, sis. What's up?" Hannah asked. "How are you feeling?"

"I'm doing okay."

"You don't sound okay. Do you need me to drive over there?"

"No, I'm okay. I just can't believe I made this mistake. And with such a jerk at that."

"Well, you know I'm here. If you need to come over and camp out at my house for a few days, you're more than welcome."

"I don't want to bother you with everything you're going through right now."

"Brit, you won't be bothering me."

"It's okay."

"Well, what did you want to ask me?"

"I've been thinking a lot over the past few weeks. I didn't do well on my paper, and I can't seem to stop crying."

You and I are one in the same, Hannah thought. "You have to try to focus on your classes, Brit."

"I'm really trying, but the pregnancy is the only thing I can think about right now."

"I understand. So, what were you going to ask me?"

"I think I want to put the baby up for adoption."

"Are you sure?"

"I don't have much of a choice."

"You might need to think through it a little longer."

"I can't give this baby a good life."

"So, is that what you wanted to ask me? What I thought about it?"

"No, I wanted to ask if you and Levi would adopt my baby," Brittany said.

Hannah froze. She pulled over into the Chevron down from the school into a parking space, her heart racing. Hannah couldn't believe what she was hearing. How was she to feel?

Wow. I don't know what to say. It may be odd raising my niece or nephew as ours, but he or she won't have to be placed in foster care—or worse. I don't want Brittany letting that fool talk her into getting rid of the baby. The best part about this, Hannah would be a mother.

"Hannah, are you there?"

"Yes...I'm here. Wow, I don't know what to say."

"Say yes."

"Brit, I would love to adopt the baby as my own. I planned to carry my own child to term, but maybe this is a blessing in disguise. Thank you for considering us. I do have to run this passed Levi. I don't know what he will say, honestly, but I'm excited. Thank you, sis!"

"Hannah, I felt so bad for you losing the baby, and then finding out you probably can't have any children. I know you and Levi would make great parents, and I'm just not ready for this. I really don't think I can give this child a good life."

Hannah felt a tear sneak down her cheek as she listened to her sister. Her heart said yes. She hoped Levi would agree. "Are you sure you don't want to think this through first?" Hannah asked.

"It's all I have thought about. I just know this is the right decision."

"Well, I'll talk to Levi as soon as he gets in, and I'll let you know something soon."

"Okay."

"And you stop worrying. I'm here for you."

"I know."

"Have you told Mama?"

"For her to make me feel worse?"

"How about we tell her together?"

"You would do that for me?" Brittany asked, her voice cracking.

"Yeah, but once you're up to it."

"Okay. I'll call her next week to see if she will be at home next Saturday. Would that work?"

"Yes. We can drive out to see her," Hannah offered, putting the car in reverse to pull out of the parking lot, continuing home.

"Okay, I'm nervous."

"Everything will be fine, Brit."

"*Ummm,* we're talking about our mama, right?"

"Yes. If she starts saying hateful things, we'll leave."

"Okay."

"Let's just think positive. Maybe we can have a real conversation with her."

"I hope for your sake she'll let down that wall she's had up for years. I want her to treat you better."

"Me too. Oh yeah, I didn't tell you about what I found," Hannah said, turning onto her street.

"I found a marriage license that shows Mama was married to a guy named Terrance Singleton. They were married when I was born. He died when I was one."

"What? I always thought that Mama was only married to me and Malik's dad."

"Apparently not," Hannah said.

"But why doesn't she still have that name?"

"That's what I said. Levi said she could've gone back to using her maiden name after his death."

"Wait a minute," Brittany stated as if she just got a revelation. "You don't think he could've been your dad..."

"I hope not."

"Have you asked Mr. Monroe?"

"I can't get up the nerve to ask. If this Terrance guy was my dad, I don't know what I'm going to do."

"Like you always tell me, it's going to be fine," Brittany said.

"I really hope so. I don't know how much more I can take, sis," Hannah replied, now sitting in her driveway.

"Hannah, think about it like this: The truth doesn't really matter because you know the man that has been *dad* to you all of your life."

"That's true," Hannah said, feeling uncomfortable with the thought.

"Your discovery may be the answer to why Mama has been so angry toward you and him."

"But I didn't ask to be a part of whatever that mess was between them."

"Just ask Mr. Monroe. Don't assume anything right now."

"I will soon."

"Okay. Let me know if you need me. Love you," Brittany said.

"Love you more," Hannah replied before disconnecting the line.

After getting settled in, Hannah went downstairs and out to the patio. She wasn't excited about the September heat, but she wanted to sit out back for a bit. The stifling heat only allowed her to remain outside for ten minutes. She then headed inside and stretched out on the couch, giving in to a much-needed nap. An hour later, Hannah was awakened by her cell phone vibrating on the coffee table. She sat up and answered it.

"I'm on my way," Levi said.

"Okay. I'm just waking up from a nap. That was some good sleep."

"You sound like it."

"Are you going to pick something up?"

"I was going to swing by Zaxby's."

"Well, bring me a house salad."

"Okay."

"Oh, I have something serious to talk to you about when you get here."

"Okay. Is everything alright?"

"Yes. It's actually some exciting news."

"Really?"

"Yes, really," Hannah said, smiling as if he could see her through the phone.

"Alright. Sounds like something we need right now. I'll be there in a bit," Levi said before hanging up.

After disconnecting the call, Hannah began to think about how Levi would take what she was getting ready to ask him. She thought long and hard about the baby and the joy he or she would bring to their life. Hannah would have never thought she would be in this situation.

Maybe we need to talk to an attorney as well. This is not just a situation of keeping the child for a few months. We would become the child's parents. This is so exciting.

Hannah's mind raced with all kinds of thoughts. She took a deep breath then she began to think about turning the office into a nursery. She opened Pinterest and searched for nursery themes.

Aww, these are so beautiful.

She pinned theme after theme. She then clicked on the T.V., logged into Hulu and watched a few episodes of *The Jeffersons*. Hannah couldn't get enough of these old shows.

Levi finally arrived, and Hannah's heart raced as she stood to shut the garage door while Levi went to put the food on the stove. Hannah then headed back over to the couch.

"I'm going to take a quick shower, then we can talk."

"Okay," Hannah said, relieved she had a few minutes to think about how she would bring up the adoption. She was too nervous, so she tried to relax by turning her attention back to the T.V. show. A few minutes into another episode, Levi came downstairs.

"Alright. Let me grab our food."

"Okay, I can't wait to share the news."

"What is it?"

"Go get the food first, then I'll tell you."

Time seemed to stand still. From the couch, she watched Levi as he poured himself some lemonade and warmed his food in the microwave. Hannah's heart rate sped up at the sound of the microwave, indicating the food was done. Levi returned to the living room a couple of minutes later.

"Okay. What's up?" he asked, placing the bag on the coffee table.

"*Ummm*, you have to have an open mind."

"Okay." Levi stated with a curious expression. "So, what's up?" he asked, taking a seat beside her.

"Well, promise me you're going to think about it."

"Think about it? Think about what? I can't promise anything until you tell me what you're talking about," Levi said. Hannah wrung her hands, struggling to speak. She wanted him to say yes.

"W–Well..." Hannah stammered.

"Why are you so nervous? What's up?"

"Brittany asked if we would adopt her baby," Hannah blurted out, searching Levi's eyes for a response.

She couldn't tell what he felt. His silence made her even more nervous. He began rubbing his head. Hannah's heart did a cartwheel. *Please say yes. Say something*. Levi continued to rub his head before speaking.

"Babe, that is a huge decision to make right now."

"I know, but do you think you would consider it? Brit believes we would be good parents for him or her. I do too."

"I don't know, Hannah. I want us to see about the treatments for you first. I wouldn't want to decide to do something like that right now."

"I think I want to try this treatment I found called Progestin-only pills, but what if it doesn't work? And I pray I don't develop some of the side effects like weight change, changes in my cycle, and other things. I want the chance at becoming a mother. This might be the answer."

"Let's think about it. Plus, Brittany also needs time to think too. That's a big decision for her as well."

"She said she's already thought about it. She wants us to adopt the baby.Plus, the baby is not due for months. That can give us time to prepare. I would rather adopt my niece or nephew as my own than adopt a child I know nothing about."

"It all sounds wonderful, babe, but let's just take some time to think about it. Brittany is very emotional right now."

"She sounded pretty sure."

"Yeah, but what happens when she sees the baby?"

"Levi, we have to think positive. If she came to us, don't you think she's thought it through?"

"Yeah, but people change their mind," Levi said, standing. He seemed to be becoming frustrated. Hannah didn't want to turn this into an argument. She hoped he would be game.

"I think it would be great because the baby wouldn't be raised by strangers."

"Yeah, but what would we tell this child? They would see their biological mom all the time. How do you think that child would feel?"

"We can cross that bridge when we come to it."

"It is not that easy, Hannah. I would love to do this, but I don't know how this all would work out."

"Well, can you think about it for me? It would allow us to be parents," Hannah said, standing and wrapping her arms around him. He felt stiff. Hannah became worried.

"I'll think about it, but don't go getting your hopes all up about the baby because you never know what could happen. I don't want you disappointed. Maybe you can try the treatment, and we can keep trying. I believe God is going to give us our own child," Levi said, wrapping his arms around her and kissing the top of her head. Hannah relaxed in his arms. She didn't doubt Levi loved her. She wanted to have hope like him, but she believed this was her opportunity to receive this precious gift. *I know being a mother would fill the empty space in my heart. This is the answer.* Hannah was sure of it. *If I get pregnant, that will be a double blessing. I've got to convince Levi.*

"Hannah," Levi stated, pulling her from her daydream.

"Yes," she replied, her head still on his chest.

"Like my mama always says, 'God can do it.' Do you believe it?"

"Maybe this is his way of doing it," Hannah said, lifting her head and kissing her husband. She noticed Levi's silence.

Hannah heard her husband, but she felt adopting Brittany's baby was God's way of *doing it* for them. She hoped Levi would soon agree. She just knew this was the glimmer of light that would begin to eliminate the darkness in her life.

CHAPTER TEN

Saturday, October 10

A few weeks had passed since Brittany's offer to adopt her baby. Hannah continued to hold out hope that Levi would agree. On Wednesday, Hannah went to see Dr. Calhoun, the infertility specialist. Instead of the Progestin-only pills, the doctor suggested starting with a combination of estrogen and progestin. They were supposed to reduce the endometriosis growth by stopping her cycle, which could help her get pregnant again. The only issue was that she had to take the pills for several months before the specialist would have her to stop them, wait for her cycle to regulate and hope for a positive pregnancy result a few months after taking them.

Hannah almost refused the treatment as the doctor explained even more of the possible side effects. She hoped she wouldn't experience any of those horrible things. She didn't want to even think about possible cancer forming. Dr. Calhoun told her the cases were small, but Hannah didn't want to be one of the statistics.

At the beginning of the month, her cycle was a few days late, so she took a home pregnancy test. It was negative. Hannah was disappointed even though she knew her condition. She didn't want to get her hopes up over and over. It was too stressful. That's why she just needed her husband to agree to the adoption. Hannah didn't want to miss the opportunity to be a mother because the thought of a long road of treatments just brought more disappointment.

Hannah and her sister were almost at their mom's. Hannah had kept her promise to go with Brittany when she was ready to tell their mom about the baby.

"What are you thinking about?" Brittany asked, pulling Hannah out of her thoughts as they neared their mom's street.

"Being able to be a mother. Thank you for offering me such a gift," Hannah said.

"I wouldn't have chosen anyone else. I've always looked up to you, sis."

"Really?"

"Yes."

"Well, thank you. I don't know why."

"I admire your strength. You've been through so much, but you keep going."

"Well, I've thought about giving up a few times over the years," Hannah stated, turning into her mom's driveway.

Their mom lived in a modest neighborhood. All of the houses were old and in need of repair. Hannah scanned the yard, her eyes landing on the unkempt flowers near the door.

Hannah hadn't been to Roswell in a few years. She had attempted to come and see her mom off and on since her college years. Her mom's response was always the same. Once she didn't show up at Hannah and Levi's wedding, Hannah hadn't tried to return.

Her heart raced as she pulled into her mom's driveway. This was the last place Hannah wanted to be, but she wanted to support her sister. Brittany had called her last week and informed Hannah that their mom said she would be home on Saturday. Hannah couldn't leave her hanging.

"Are you ready?" she asked Brittany.

"I guess."

"Let's get this over with."

Hannah and Brittany exited the car and walked a few steps to the door. Her heartbeat seemed to increase as Brittany knocked on the door, which used to be black, but a lot of the paint had chipped and what was left was a dull grayish color. No one answered at first, so Brittany knocked louder.

"Who is it?" her mom yelled from a distance.

"It's Brittany and Hannah," Brittany replied.

Hannah gave Brittany an *oh, boy* look as they awaited the storm that would soon come. Moments later, her mom snatched open the front door and walked away. Hannah looked at Brittany.

"I guess that means come in," Brittany said.

"After you," Hannah said.

Hannah stepped in behind her sister and closed the door. She followed Brittany's lead and took a seat on the sofa. The small living room space was clean. The fabric chairs were fading, and a ton of angelic figurines still sat on the shelf in the corner near the small kitchen. *Nothing has changed,* Hannah thought, taking it all in. Their mom had taken a seat in the old cushioned rocker near the dated TV. She sat staring at Hannah and Brittany.

"Hey, Mama," Brittany began.

"Hey," she muttered.

"We came by to see you and talk with you."

"Hey, Mama," Hannah said, her voice shaking.

"Ummm. You finally remembered you have a mama I guess," her mom said, rolling her eyes.

"Mama, how are you?" Brittany interjected.

"I'm fine. What do you want to talk about?"

"Well, I have something to tell you," Brittany said, sitting on the couch. Hannah followed suit.

"What?" her mom stated with irritation. Hannah noticed the beer can on the floor next to the chair.

"I–I'm pregnant."

"Ummm," grunted their mom. "I don't know why you're telling me. You got it. You raise it. I told y'all I ain't rocking no babies."

"Mama, I wanted you to know."

"Okay, you told me. You're twenty years old. I can't help you. I don't know how you plan to finish school."

"I plan to, Mama," Brittany said. Hannah sat and listened. She was there for moral support.

"How, Brit? You can't have no baby on campus. You g'on have to get your own place I guess because you can't come back here. You knew you couldn't take care of no baby. Y'all girls have never been nothing but a headache in my life."

Hannah's shoulders stiffened. *Mama did not just say that to us. Who says that to their own children?* "Mama, your daughter came out here to tell you something very difficult, and you tell her and me that we've been nothing but headaches," Hannah stated, fuming. She slid closer to Brittany, hugging her as her sister sobbed, her head on Hannah's shoulder.

"That's what I said. You two have been a constant headache. And she ain't coming back in here."

"I don't have to. Hannah and Levi are going to take the baby," Brittany blurted out hysterically, then lay her head back on Hannah's shoulder.

"Brittany?" Hannah whispered, wishing her sister had not spilled that information.

"Oh, yeah? And how is that going to work with your sister raising your child–her niece or nephew? And why are you and your husband being so nice, taking on somebody else's responsibility?" their mom spewed in Hannah's direction.

"I just don't get it," Hannah stated. She had to know.

"Get what?" her mom asked, taking a big gulp from the beer can.

"Mama, I wasn't going to say anything, but I have to ask this question," Hannah said.

"Ask me what?"

"Who is Terrance Singleton–or was Terrance Singleton?"

"Why?" her mom spat.

"I would like to know."

"He was my first husband."

"Why was I born while you two were married?"

"Girl, don't come up in my house questioning me."

"Tell me the truth," Hannah yelled.

"Who do you think you're talking to?"

"Mama, I'm not trying to disrespect you, but I need to know. Who was Terrance?"

"I told you who he was. I was married to him. We separated for a short time, and I met your raggedy, no-good daddy, got pregnant with you and…" her mom stated, her words trailing off.

"And?" Hannah stated firmly.

Her mom sat quietly for a couple of minutes. Brittany continued to sob. Hannah stood and moved closer to her mom, who was staring at the TV screen, which was turned all the way down. Hannah knew she was trying to avoid her question. "And?" Hannah asked again.

"And he left me because of you."

"Because of me?"

"Yea, because of you."

"But I didn't do anything. I was a baby. You're not making since, Mama."

"I'm making plenty of sense. I got hooked up with your sorry daddy. Soon, my husband wanted to get back together, but I was pregnant with you, so....," Hannah's mom trailed off again.

"So, what?"

"So, I told him you were his."

"You did what?" Hannah asked, not believing what she was hearing.

"You heard me, and soon after that, we would argue a lot. One night, he got drunk, left home, and died in a car accident."

"Mama, I'm sorry that happened, but I'm not to blame for it. I was an innocent child."

"You are to blame. You and your sorry daddy," her mom screamed, standing, her words slurring. Hannah backed away.

"I'm not to blame for a choice you made. Is that why you've treated me so bad over the years?" Hannah asked. More silence. Then, her mother turned and walked into the kitchen. Hannah followed her.

"Mama," Hannah said.

"Why don't you just get out and take your sister with you."

"Really?" Hannah asked.

"Yes," her mom replied, taking what looked like leftovers from the refrigerator and setting the pot on the gas stove.

"Mama, why won't you talk to me?" Hannah asked, moving closer to her again.

"Sis, let's just go," Brittany said, standing next to Hannah now. "I'm not going to be anybody's disappointment. I'm tired of Mama mistreating you and me. We are your daughters," Brittany screamed, walking toward her mom. Their mom turned around and glared at Brittany without speaking.

"Mama, I've always loved and wanted a relationship with you," Hannah said, now in tears. Her mom turned back toward the stove, turning it on.

"Don't cry, sis," Brittany said, turning and hugging Hannah now. "I'm here for you."

"How're you going to be there for somebody, and you done went and got yourself pregnant? I thought you were going to make something out of yourself. I guess I can only depend on my son to do that."

Brittany spun around. "I don't know why Hannah tries with you. I don't know why I try. Hannah made something out of herself, but you disregard her like she's nothing to you. You act like you hate us, Mama. Let's just go, Hannah," Brittany finally said.

"Mama, did you hear, Brittany?" Hannah asked. Her mom still wouldn't look at them, reaching in the utensil drawer and pulling out a large spoon. "Mama do you hate us?" Hannah asked. Still no response.

"I guess you answered my question," Brittany said, making her way to the front door. Hannah turned and walked back into the living room, grabbed her keys off the couch and headed to the door. Then, she turned and walked back to the kitchen entrance to look at her mom again. Her mom still refused to look at her. Hannah wanted to share the loss of the baby with her. She wanted her mom to walk over and wrap her arms around her and tell her everything would be fine. She wanted her mom to tell her she loved her, and she didn't blame her for her mistakes. That was Hannah's greatest desire, but it wasn't happening today, maybe never.

Hannah and Brittany left their mom's house as quick as they came. Hannah couldn't wait to get away from there. She unlocked the doors, and she and Brittany climbed in. Hannah sped off and didn't slow down until she was on the highway. She and Brittany rode in silence for several miles. Hannah wanted this *nightmare* of a life to be over.

"Are you okay?" Brittany finally asked.

"Not really."

"Me either. I want Mama to let go of all of that hate she feels."

"I do too," Hannah said.

"I see I can't depend on her at all. I just hope to finish college and be able to take care of myself someday soon."

"You will."

"I really thought that me and Travis would do things right and get married first, start our careers and then have children. I shouldn't have fallen for his pressure to sleep together."

"Don't beat yourself up. You haven't really had the best example. We both have to move forward with our lives."

"You're right. I really hope Levi will agree to the adoption."

"Me too," Hannah said. She was looking forward to her life getting better, but then this nonsense with her mom. Since they were on that side of town, Hannah decided to stop by her dad's house. She really needed to talk to him.

"Brit, do you mind if I stop in Norcross at Daddy's place before we head back home?"

"Girl, you know I love Mr. Monroe. Let's go. I don't have any exams coming up, so I don't have to rush back to the dorms."

"Okay. Let me make sure he's there," Hannah said, pulling her phone from her purse, opening her recent call log, and pressing on her dad's name. He answered on the second ring. "Hey, Daddy."

"Hey. What's up?"

"Are you at home? I'm headed your way."

"Yes. I'm off today. Come on. I would love to see you. What brought you out this way?"

"Brittany and I went over to see Mama, but not for long."

"Oh, boy. What happened?"

"I have to explain when we get there. I also need you to tell me more about what went on between you and Mama when she was married to Terrance Singleton."

"How do you know about that?" Hannah's dad asked, sounding nervous.

"I stumbled on the marriage license when I was checking out ancestry.com online."

"Well, I guess we'll be having a long talk when you get here."

"Yes, we will. Looking at that stuff made me wonder if that man was my daddy. Why didn't you tell me?"

"I was ashamed, sweetheart. We had an affair."

"Yeah, Mama told me, but I wish you would have, then, I would have understood more of why she was so angry toward me and you."

"That's not something you tell your young child."

"I guess."

"I've got the feeling your mama told her side of the story."

"I don't believe she told me everything. She just dragged you through the mud as usual."

"I'm sure, but I won't speak negatively about your mama. I'll tell you everything."

"Okay, Daddy. We should be there in about thirty minutes."

"Okay, sounds good. I love you, sweetheart."

"I love you too. I really appreciate you," Hannah finally said before hanging up.

CHAPTER ELEVEN

Saturday, October 17

Even though Hannah had only been on the estrogen and progestin combination for about a week, she was still determined to search for natural alternatives. She sat on the patio with her laptop, enjoying the peace and quiet before their house became crowded and noisy. Levi had gotten some of their family to agree to a barbecue. Hannah was still not really up to talking. Her mind had been on her mom and her conversation with her dad. He had told her more of the details of his relationship with her mom. It had broken Hannah's heart to hear that her mom was still angry and blamed Hannah's birth for the death of her first husband, Terrance.

Her parents had an affair, and her mom got pregnant with her while she and Terrance were apart. Later, Terrance wanted them to work it out, so her mom broke it off with Hannah's dad. That's when Hannah guessed her mom try to keep up her story about Hannah being his. Hannah's dad said he met with her to talk about how they would work together to care for Hannah. Apparently, someone who knew Terrance overheard their conversation, and based on her mom, they had an argument, and he died in a car accident afterwards.

Hannah rubbed her temples, trying not to burst into tears. She was tired of crying. She shook off the thoughts and tried to focus on what she was doing and hoping Levi would finally say yes to the adoption.

So far, she had read up on beta-carotene and increasing fatty acids. She was now reading about something called N-acetyl cysteine. It had been recognized for helping those with endometriosis and also reduced cysts.

"Well, that's a two-for-one," Hannah said, sending the article to her email.

"Babe, what are you doing?" Levi asked, walking up behind her and kissing her neck.

"I'm still doing my research. I don't know how long I'll take that other stuff. It just has way too many side effects."

"I agree. It looks like you found something," Levi said, reading the computer screen.

"Yeah. I want to read up on it a little more later."

"Sounds like a plan."

"Did you think about Brittany's offer?" Hannah blurted out, unable to hold the question any longer. She needed him to say yes.

"I've really been thinking about it."

"Can you say yes, please?"

"Can you let me get my words out?"

Hannah's heart pounded. *Please say yes.*

Levi grabbed her arm and looked into her eyes. "Hannah, this has been hard with us losing our child. I want you to know that I am here to walk with you through this endometriosis diagnosis. We are *one*. That's one thing Dad taught me."

"And?" Hannah said, her anxiety rising.

"We're going to continue to trust God because I believe we are going to have more than one child to love and care for."

Hannah's heart raced. *Is he talking about after my treatments?* "What are you saying?"

"Didn't you hear me? We are going to be parents."

"Huh?"

"Did you forget that quick? We'll be adopting Brittany's baby."

"Oh, so that's a yes?"

"Yes." Levi smiled.

"Thank you. We'll be great parents, you just wait," Hannah said, jumping up and down, wiping away tears of joy.

"I know we will."

"I promise to keep trying the treatments, and who knows, we may have a whole football team."

"Oh, wait now. Pump your brakes," Levi said, and he and Hannah laughed. She was filled with excitement. "But seriously, I thought about it more and more, and I think we should go through with it."

"That's so great to hear," Hannah stated, feeling as if a weight had been lifted off of her shoulder. She placed her laptop back on the patio table and grabbed her husband's face, kissing him tenderly. *Thank you, Lord.* "I love you."

"I love you too," Levi replied, smiling as they enjoyed each other's embrace.

A few minutes later, they both headed inside. Levi went into the kitchen to make preparations for their barbecue, and Hannah headed up to their bedroom, taking two steps at a time.

I can't wait to tell Brittany.

Once she entered their room, she sprinted over to the nightstand and grabbed her phone. Hannah's fingers had never moved so fast. She waited for her sister to answer. She lay across the bed and clicked on the TV. Brittany finally picked up. She and her sister cheered through the phone after Hannah gave her the good news. They chatted for a few minutes. Brittany told her she would see her when she got there. After hanging up, Hannah lay down and took a nap.

About thirty minutes later, Hannah turned toward the bay window in the corner of their bedroom. That was her second favorite place in the house. She loved coming in from a long day and resting on the small bench in front of it. Some days she would just recline on the plush pillows and close her eyes. Hannah admired the sun's rays on this beautiful Saturday afternoon. It was now noon, but she pulled the covers up to her chin. She lay resting a little while longer. Their house would soon be flooded with friends and relatives. Levi had invited her dad, his mom, Brittany, Robin and a few others. Uncle Joseph and Aunt Melissa were out of town celebrating their anniversary. Hannah wanted to assist with the preparations, but Levi had insisted on doing it all. He loved to *throw down* on the grill. Those were his words. It felt odd to not help, so Hannah soon went downstairs to straighten up the living room area a little. She was dusting the fireplace and end tables when the door chimed. Levi was bringing in bags from the store.

"Do you need any help?" Hannah asked.

"I told you I would get it all done. Go relax."

"Levi, you know I have to help with something."

"No, you don't have to. I'm good," Levi said with a grin.

"Okay, okay." Hannah went back upstairs and climbed back onto the bed.

She grabbed her phone, placed her feet slightly under the covers and turned on her audiobook, laying her head back on their leather headboard. Hannah was almost done with her third novel. She tried listening but found herself searching Pinterest for more baby ideas. She then searched Walmart's website, looking at baby clothes. Bored, Hannah soon drifted back to sleep.

A few minutes later, Hannah heard her dad's voice yelling over the vacuum cleaner. Still excited, Hannah decided to go downstairs and tell her dad about the adoption. She and Brittany had told him about the baby last weekend and about how her mom had responded. Hannah just loved her dad. Feeling embarrassed again, Brittany had burst into to tears again at his house. He walked over and wrapped his arms around her sister as if she were his daughter too.

As she opened the door to their bedroom, Hannah smiled at him as he vacuumed the living room carpet. She then smiled at the thought of the two wonderful men in her life. Her dad looked up.

"Hey, sweetheart. Did I wake you?"

"Hey, Daddy. No, you didn't. I needed to get up."

"Well, I won't argue with that. It's late. You know I get up with the chickens."

"Really, Daddy. The chickens." Hannah shook her head as she descended the stairs.

"Yeah, girlfriend," he stated, trying to sound hip.

"*Ummm,* Daddy. Don't say that again," Hannah responded with a giggle, now at the bottom of the stairs with her hands on her hips, trying to look serious. Levi burst into laughter, looking over at them, then he disappeared through the patio door.

"Are you calling me old again on the sly?"

"No, not on the sly. Up close and personal. I mean you are getting up there. You are, in your words, 'knocking on sixty's door.'" Hannah gave her dad a big hug. "You know I love you, though."

"I love you too, baby girl. Don't make me take my belt off. I'm only fifty-four."

"A belt, Daddy? I'm way too old for that. And as I said, sixty is peeking around the corner. See it. Look." Hannah pointed at the corner near the downstairs bathroom. They both burst into laughter.

Hannah stepped over to the sliding glass door. Looking to the left, she saw Levi trying to light the grill. She smiled as he put his finger in his mouth, obviously hurting from so many attempts.

Turning back to her dad, she waited for him to finish vacuuming. As she watched him wind the cord and place the vacuum back into the downstairs closet, she cleared her throat to get his attention.

"Sweetheart, everything okay?" he asked, walking over to the loveseat and taking a seat across from her.

"Yes. I'm good, Daddy. I do have something to share with you."

"Oh yeah. What's up?"

"You know I've been doing some research on different treatments for endometriosis..."

"That's good. Have you found anything?"

"I did start one a little over a week ago."

"Okay. Sounds like a plan. It'll work out. You just wait and see. I'll be a grandad sooner than you think."

"Well, you're right, Dad."

"What do you mean?"

"We're going to adopt."

"Oh, really?"

"Yeah."

"Well, there are many children in the world who need a loving couple like you and Levi in their life."

"I agree, but the baby we're going to adopt is..."

"Is?" Hannah's dad repeated, moving to the edge of the loveseat.

"Well, Brittany is..."

"Yea, I really wish she would have waited until she got married and established before motherhood."

"Yeah. You know she was broken up about that. Then, we told you what Mama said to her."

"Yeah. Sad. She really needs her."

"Well, she came to me and asked if Levi and I would adopt the baby."

"Really?"

"Yes."

"Are you comfortable with that, sweetheart?"

"Yes. I have to admit I'm a little nervous about raising my niece or nephew as my own, but I'm so excited to have the opportunity to be a mom."

"I think it's a great idea. The baby won't be raised by strangers."

"Yes! Plus, Brittany can see him or her as well."

"Now, what about telling the child the truth someday?" her dad asked.

"Yeah. I've thought about that."

"I just advise you all not to keep the truth from him or her as they grow to an age of understanding."

"Thank you for that, Daddy."

"I pray things go well. Also, don't give up on God sending your own miracle," he replied, standing to give her a hug.

"I love you, Daddy."

"I love you too. Remember, I'm still here, even if you're married now. I'm here for both you and Levi."

"I know. Thank you for being a great dad."

"By God's grace."

"Alright. I'm going to go up and get myself together for this little shindig," Hannah stated, moving toward the stairs.

"Alright. Let's get ready to turn up," her dad stated, cutting a step.

"Daddy, stop."

"Girl, I can groove."

"Whatever," Hannah replied, laughing as she ascended the stairs.

Her dad nodded and smiled up at her, pumping his hands in the air to his imaginary music. She shook her head. *He is so crazy.*

By two o'clock, everyone had arrived. Hannah loved on her mother-in-law when she walked in. She was an amazing woman. About Hannah's height, she was always glamorous, not overdressed but just enough to turn heads. At age sixty-one, she could still go for at least fifty. Mama Jefferson was dressed in a pair of jeans with a purple top. She was blinged out with her matching jewelry and hat. Hannah admired how she had pressed on after her husband's death just two years ago. Levi was always worried about her. She was glad she lived nearby. Levi's friend Quinton and his wife were also able to make it. Quinton and Levi had been friends since they were kids. They grew up in the same neighborhood and attended the same elementary and middle school.

Everyone sat out back on the patio. It had turned out to be a beautiful October afternoon. The temperature was just right for an outdoor activity. And there was a light breeze. The smell from the barbecue grill made Hannah's stomach growl. Hannah and Mama Jefferson played a round of Uno while her dad, Robin, Quinton and his wife played a game of spades. Hannah enjoyed every moment of the game and laughing with Mama Jefferson.

"Man, I can't wait to dig in. That grill smells great. I haven't had much of an appetite lately," Hannah stated.

"Yes, it does," her mother-in-law concurred. "You do have a keeper, sweetheart, and I'm not just saying that because he's my son."

"Thanks, Mama. You and Mr. Jefferson did a great job. Levi is a great husband, if I must say so myself."

"All credit to God, sweetheart."

As they played, they chatted a bit more. Hannah looked over at Brittany. She noticed how silent she had been. Brittany sat off to herself across from them at the table that housed the condiments and paper goods. Hannah stood with Brittany looking up at her.

"Hey, what's going on with you? You look out of it."

"I'm good. I'm just worried about what everyone will say once I really start showing."

"You can't worry about that, Brit."

"I try not to."

"Come on over and get ready for some of this good barbecue."

"Okay," Brittany said, smiling. "Sis, thank you for being here for me. I hate that we missed so many years together."

"Me too," Hannah replied. "And as I always tell you, I'm proud of you. That hasn't changed. It takes a strong woman to make such a difficult decision as you have, and I promise to do an excellent job with our little one."

"Thank you, sis."

"Alright, come on," Hannah said, grabbing Brittany's hand and some paper plates off the table. Hannah dragged Brittany over with her to see how the spade game was going first. They joked with Quinton and her dad because Robin and his wife were winning. Her dad pretended to be mad saying they were traders. Quinton's wife had never really been a big talker, but she was a sweetheart. Leaving that table, they headed back to where Hannah sat with Mama Jefferson. After a few more minutes, they headed toward the other end of the table, where Levi was placing a pan of chicken, hot off the grill.

"Girl, you got a good man. I thought Travis was a good guy."

"Thanks, sis. Hopefully Travis will come around. At least apologize to you."

After getting their food, it was silent for a few minutes as everyone stuffed their faces. Hannah motioned for Levi to sit down and eat as well. He was still asking if anyone needed anything. He made his plate and sat next to Hannah and Mama Jefferson. Levi then leaned over and pulled Hannah close. He kissed her as if no one else was around. Hannah's body warmed. She loved this man. He was all she could've ever wanted in a husband.

"What was that for?" she asked Levi.

"Just because," he replied, smiling at her.

"Son, you outdid yourself today," Mama Jefferson stated.

"Thanks, Mama. I just wanted to have a get-together. It's been a while. I know Hannah and I have only been married two years, but I want this to take place often. I wish Pops could be here."

"Me too, son. I would love to hang out with you and Hannah more," Mama Jefferson replied.

"If you keep cooking like this, I'll be over every weekend. You know we don't eat like this at the campus cafeteria," Brittany teased with a smirk. They all laughed. Hannah squeezed her sister's hand.

"I agree, Brittany. I won't have to cook. I can just come get my plate and hang out with my son-in-law and daughter. A two-for-one special." Hannah's dad laughed.

They all continued eating and enjoying the beautiful day and each other. Hannah took it all in. She smiled, scanning the table. Hannah realized she was truly blessed, and the new baby would be a welcomed addition. As their backyard filled with laughter and Hannah's table started a new Uno game, Hannah suddenly felt sad, wanting her mom to be a part of this circle of love.

CHAPTER TWELVE

❖

Six Months Later

After work on Tuesday evening, Hannah and Levi headed over to Home Depot. Spring was one of Hannah's favorite and worse times of year. The temperature was warm enough for them to enjoy the sun during the day and cool enough to turn off the air at night. What Hannah didn't like was her sinuses going crazy because everything was blooming, so she had to resume her daily Zyrtec to help manage her seasonal allergies. She and Levi climbed out of the car and walked hand in hand, excited about becoming parents. As they strolled across the parking lot from their car to the door, Hannah drew closer to her husband and lay her head on his shoulder. Looking up at him, she once again thanked him for saying yes to the adoption and for being the man of her dreams.

The past few months had been like a roller coaster. Hannah's emotions had been up and down as she battled through another endometriosis treatment. Due to the side effects of severe headaches and swelling in her legs, the specialist switched Hannah to Progestin-only pills. Hannah was also trying a few natural remedies. The painful cramps had decreased, but her cycle was all over the place, and she had also gained ten pounds.

Before meeting with Dr. Calhoun about her issues, Hannah had taken numerous pregnancy tests, which were all negative. For the past few months, she would make a run to the pharmacy a few blocks away from their house because her cycle was so unpredictable. A few times, weeks would pass before it started. Of course, it was due to the treatment. Hannah was tired of the stress that came with her physical health, not to mention the drama with her mom for what seemed like every week since her and Brittany's visit. Her mom had threatened to remove Brittany from her insurance after she got a few small bills. Hannah and Levi helped Brittany pay for them.

Then, her mom had tried to talk Brittany out of her allowing them to adopt the baby, saying it was going to be a mess. Hannah had grown tired of all of it. She was thankful that Brittany hadn't changed her mind. She finally decided to focus on the adoption and becoming the best mom she could be, regardless if she carried the baby in her womb or not.

Last month, she, Levi, and Brittany had met with their attorney who specialized in adoptions. They had started the consent to adopt paperwork, which Brittany had agreed upon. They only needed to get the same consent from Travis after the DNA test once the baby was born. Travis had told Brittany he would consent. The adoption paperwork, which was the legal paperwork that would list them as the parents, last month. Hannah was grateful that the state of Georgia only required the consent of both parents in relative adoptions, and there weren't loads of paperwork or other requirements. She had learned that after doing a little research on the process.

Now, Hannah stood staring at the paint samples and waiting for Levi to return from grabbing some new cabinet knobs for the kitchen. She was torn between the peach and pink for the nursery. Brittany was now twenty-nine weeks, and Hannah and Levi had decided it was time to convert the office into a nursery. Hannah couldn't wait for their little one to arrive.

"Babe, look at these," Levi said from behind her.

Hannah jumped. "You scared me, man."

"I'm sorry. Check out these silver knobs. I like the style of them. What do you think?" Levi asked, holding up a straight silver bar. It looked like the ones found on stoves, only thinner and much nicer.

"I like them too."

"Good. I hope I grabbed enough. Did you figure out which color you want for our little princess?"

"I was looking at this peach color for the wall and maybe mix in some mint green with the items for the crib. But I also like this soft pink."

"How about we do something different since pink is like the standard color for a girl's nursery."

"That's true. We'll go with the peach then."

"Sounds good," Levi said, telling the guy they were ready for him to mix the paint.

They walked around for a few minutes, admiring the light fixtures and other household items before returning for their paint and making their way to checkout. As the cashier rang up their items, Hannah turned to face Levi, clapped lightly and giggled. "I'm so excited. The past few months have been torture for me."

"I know they have. The little one will be a blessing in our lives."

"I know she will," Hannah said. They had found out the gender at Brittany's five-month checkup.

"Do you want to stop and grab some dinner–I mean, sit down and enjoy each other's company for a change?" Levi said.

"That's sounds good. Where do you want to stop?"

"Nothing big. How about Los Broncos, that Mexican restaurant up the street from here?"

"Okay. I'm in the mood for a chicken fajita."

"Well, let's go then."

After securing the paint in the container Levi carried in the trunk for work, they headed over to Los Broncos. Because it was a weeknight, there were few cars in the parking lot. Hannah was grateful to be out of the house and spending time with Levi. Pulling into one of the many parking spaces, they exited the car, locked arms and made their way inside. Hannah looked around at the nearly empty place while they waited for a waitress to take them to a table.

They asked to be seated in a booth in the back. After taking their seats, Levi and Hannah began talking about possible names for the baby.

"I think I like Winnie," Levi said, trying to keep a straight face.

"*Ummm,* you mean like Winnie the Pooh? I think not."

"What if I meant like Winnie Mandela?"

"Still a no."

"Okay, what about Ocean?" Levi asked, bursting into laughter.

"Stop playing," Hannah said, hitting the top of his hand lightly.

"Okay, okay," Levi said before the older Hispanic woman walked over to take their drink orders. Hannah was still laughing when she walked away.

"I was thinking something like Neveah or Gabrielle."

"Babe, those are beautiful names."

"Which one do you like best?" Hannah asked.

"I would probably say Neveah."

"That one's my favorite too."

"So, do you think Travis is going to try anything stupid to stop the adoption?"

"I don't think so. Brit said he just wanted to get it over with."

"Wow, so selfish. I hope he doesn't cause any extra stress like your mama"

"Right. I hope Mama will stop with her nonsense too," Hannah replied.

"You know, even though you told me what her and Pops shared with you, I still don't get how your mama could hold a grudge toward you like that. I'm so sorry, babe."

"Are you guys ready to order?" the waitress asked.

"Yes," they said in unison.

"Alright, well, what are you having this evening?"

"Yes, I would like a taco salad with beef with all the toppings," Levi said, turning over the menu as if getting ready to order more.

"Is that it, sir?"

"*Ummm,* yes," he finally said, scanning the menu once more.

"And for you, young lady?"

"I want one large fajita with rice and beans with chicken and mild salsa on the side."

"Is that all?"

"Yes," Hannah said.

"Alright. I'll get this right in for you two."

"Thanks," Hannah replied.

"Yeah, like I was saying, I still don't get your mom. That's not cool," Levi said, sliding closer to Hannah, putting his arm around her.

"I don't either. If you could have seen her when we tried to get her to look at us that day. I think she's been through more than what happened between her and Daddy."

"It's possible."

"Levi, I grew up wanting Mama in my life. My spirit was broken even more when Malcolm molested me and she—my own mama—didn't believe me and took up for him and Aunt Loretta."

"Yeah, I still want to pull up at his house right now."

"You can't pull up at their house. I don't want you losing your freedom or job over him."

"I told you I can pay somebody to bruise him up a bit," Levi joked. "But seriously, babe, I pray your mom comes around one day. She's missed out on a lot in your life. She has so much to be proud of."

"I hope she does too. The miscarriage, endometriosis and wanting to build a relationship with her have been a lot on my shoulders. I just want to focus on being a better mother to our child than she has been to me."

"I agree, but I'm glad you're at least talking about it more. I remember a time you internalized everything."

"I know. It still hurts to talk about it. I longed to tell her so many things over the years. Now, I don't know if that relationship will ever happen," Hannah said, trying to pull her vibrating phone from her purse. It was a message from Brittany.

Hey, sis. Sorry to bother you.

I keep getting messages from Mama. She sounds like she gets when she is drinking. She keeps talking about how letting you and Levi adopt the baby is going to cause all kinds of drama in my life. She keeps saying that I'll have to see the baby all the time, yet she keeps telling me how I can't come back to her house with a baby, and maybe I need to go live with my sorry daddy too. This is crazy!

"Babe, who's that?"

"It's Brittany. We spoke too soon. Mama is at it again."

"What's she doing now?" Levi asked. Hannah handed him her cell phone to read Brittany's message. "She needs to stop this."

"She really does. Brittany doesn't need this stress."

"She doesn't. Hopefully your mama doesn't keep pressing and she changes her mind."

Hannah froze at her husband's words. "That can't happen. She promised to allow us to become the baby's parents. I just want this next month to fly by so I can hold my sweet girl."

"I didn't say it would. I just said hopefully it won't."

"I have to call her and talk to her, keep her encouraged, and let her know that we won't disappoint her."

"Babe, I know you're nervous, but you also have to think about how Brittany feels at the moment. I want this baby as much as you do. Let's just remember to show some empathy when it comes to Brittany," Levi said.

"I know. I just want the adoption to be done." Hannah said just as the waitress returned to the table with their food.

Suddenly, Hannah wasn't as hungry as before. She couldn't take her mind off yet another message with her mom trying to crush her spirit. Only this time, it was an attempt to rip away the one thing Hannah planned to be much better at, a selfless mother.

CHAPTER THIRTEEN

Saturday, April 12

Amuch-needed weekend had arrived, and Hannah pulled into the parking lot in front of Ms. Priscilla's shop. Her hair was in need of some TLC. She had arrived early, so she sat in the car and waited. Ten minutes later, Hannah saw Ms. Priscilla pull up in her blue older modeled Honda Accord. She waved at her and the other stylists entering the shop. Hannah gave them a few minutes to get settled before heading inside. As a teacher, she knew how it could be to be bum-rushed before having a moment to breathe.

Hannah finally got out. The door chimed as it opened and closed to make them aware they had a visitor. She was excited to tell Ms. P about the adoption, her light in her current darkness. She also wanted to talk to her about the drama with her mom. Ms. Priscilla was in the back when Hannah walked in. Ms. Angela, a woman in her early fifties who could go for thirty-five or forty, stood at her chair parting her client's hair. Hannah said hello. Ms. Angela greeted her with a smile. She headed over to Ms. Priscilla's chair, grabbing a few magazines from the sitting area before sitting down.

Ms. Angela turned her chair to face Hannah. She had started putting in a relaxer. Her client seemed to be older as well, maybe in her late fifties. Hannah smiled and waved at the woman, who was frowning as Ms. Angela parted the section of her hair.

She must be tender headed.

"How have you been?" Ms. Angela asked.

"I've been okay," Hannah replied.

"Priscilla told me you lost the baby."

"I did. It's been hard."

"I hate to hear that. I'll keep you and your husband in my prayers."

"Thanks," Hannah replied, not wanting to talk anymore about her miscarriage.

"God will give you another one. You just wait and see."

"I know," Hannah said. *He already has in his own way.*

"Let me know if you need anything. Don't hesitate."

"I will."

As they continued chatting, Ms. Priscilla came from the back room and headed over to Hannah. Ms. Priscilla, also an older woman, appeared as if she wasn't feeling her best.

"Good morning, Ms. P," Hannah said cheerfully.

"Hi, sweetheart. How are you doing today?"

"I'm doing well."

"That's good to hear. How's that mighty man of God?"

"Who, Levi?"

"Yes, your husband. Who else would I be talking about?"

"Oh, he's good. He had to work today."

"Well, tell him I said hello."

"Yes, ma'am," Hannah replied.

Ms. Priscilla reached in her drawer and pulled out a black apron. As she put it on, Hannah noticed the pink letters that read *Blessed, and you can't do nothing about it.*

That must be new, Hannah thought. She admired Ms. Priscilla's attitude about life. Ms. Priscilla would surely say it was because of her faith. Hannah thought about their many conversations. The words on her apron would definitely describe her. She had spoken so many words of encouragement into Hannah's life for sure. Hannah had noticed something different about Ms. Priscilla from the moment they'd met. She was so loving, and she had such trust in God. She had shared her testimony with Hannah many times. She had gone through so much.

"Are you still getting a wash and trim?" Ms. Priscilla asked, breaking into Hannah's thoughts.

"Yes. I need one."

Ms. P began to prepare Hannah for a shampoo. She put plastic under the towel in case the water flowed out of the bowl. Hannah loved how she paid such attention to detail. Ms. Priscilla asked Hannah to meet her over at the sink. Hannah closed her eyes and relaxed as Ms. P massaged her scalp.

Hannah was at the shop for about three hours. She didn't realize so much time had passed. Hannah talked to Ms. Priscilla about everything. She opened up about her experiences growing up, the drama with her mom and her desire to have a relationship with her, then, she finally told her about the adoption and how she believed the baby would fill the void she'd had in her heart for so many years. Ms. Priscilla stopped for a few moments as if she was praying.

"You've been through a lot, sweetheart. Don't let those things keep you from God or forgiving those that hurt you. Your mama is hurting too. I'm not making an excuse for how she has treated you. You both have to deal with the hurt in your hearts. You can't keep covering it up."

"How, Ms. P?"

"God wants you to hand it to him now and let him heal you. Adopting your sister's baby won't fulfill you. Your husband can't do it. Neither can reconnecting with yo' mama. Only God can heal and restore you, sweetheart."

"Ms. P, to be totally honest, I don't really know how to trust God. For so many years, I've felt he was so far away from me. I accepted Christ as a teen, went to church, was part of the youth ministry, went to counseling and all, but I never stopped thinking about why he had allowed me to be abused and Mama's mistreatment. For years, I tried to forget about everything. Now, all of this drama. My mama is still drinking and blames me for her getting pregnant with me while she was married. I just don't kn..." Hannah's voice trailed off.

"You don't know what, sweetheart?"

"If God loves me or if he's punishing me. My aunt Loretta, Mama's sister, once told me not to question God."

"Don't question God? What? That's crazy talk. He's the one with the answers. Maybe she meant questioning God in your own wisdom. You know there are some out there that think they're smarter than God. I know that's not what you meant."

"No, ma'am. I just want to ask about why I've had to endure so much."

"Sweetheart, you have to talk to God like you're talking to me. He'll answer you and heal your heart."

"What do you mean?"

"You find a quiet place in the house and just open your mouth and talk to him. He's waiting on you. He knows all about it. He knew you before you were formed. He loves you more than any one can."

"I don't know about that, Ms. Priscilla," Hannah said with frustration.

"Hannah, sweetheart," Ms. Priscilla stated, turning the chair to face her. "I hear your pain, but please know God didn't cause it."

"He didn't protect me, Ms. P, and now I just feel as if he is punishing me. How can I trust him?"

"Now, I know what God was showing me when you first came into the shop."

"Huh?" Hannah asked, looking up.

"The first time you walked into the shop, God showed me a vision of a girl, maybe about fifth grade, kneeling in a corner crying. That little girl was you. I hear that little girl now as you're speaking."

"Ms. P, I'm a grown woman."

"Yes, in appearance, but in some ways, you've remained that little girl."

"I don't get what you're saying."

"Sweetie, sometimes we go through hard times. Whenever it happened, we remained right there—never able to get passed that point."

"Oh," Hannah mumbled.

"Now, you have to be healed from that place. You have to gain the strength to rise up and be the woman God created you to be."

"I'm doing what I was created to do."

"I mean in the spirit. The horrible things that have happened to you have broken your spirit. You have to be healed and trust him with your whole heart. You have to want him more than anything else, baby. With God's strength, you will rise up and help other girls and women get passed their pain. We go through and come out so we can help someone else along the way, but we have to surrender and trust God to heal those broken places."

"I don't know if I'm ready for that."

"You don't know if you're ready to be healed?"

"No. That's not what I meant. I'm not sure if I'm ready to trust God with everything, especially with my heart."

"Hannah, you'll never find contentment anywhere else. We can't cover up our pain with the things we believe will make us happy."

"Wow," was all Hannah could get out.

"He's an amazing God. I've tried him for myself," Ms. Priscilla said, cutting a step.

Hannah pasted on a smile, but her heart was heavy. She couldn't let go of the words *you have to want him more than anything else*. It never dawned on her that she wanted other things more than God.

"Thank you, Ms. P."

"No problem. That's what I'm here for. You think I just do hair? No, ma'am. I use this as an opportunity to lead someone to the one who has been with me every step of the way."

Thirty more minutes had passed, and Ms. Priscilla was almost done with Hannah's hair. She had been sitting quietly for the past few minutes pondering Ms. Priscilla's words. After finishing the last set of curls, Ms. Priscilla turned Hannah around to look in the mirror. She loved how much her hair had grown and how healthy it was. She would enjoy this press for at least a week, maybe two if she kept it wrapped and tied up at night. Then, she would be back to her naturally curly hair, which she preferred. Hannah stared at her reflection a little longer and blinked rapidly. She could have sworn she saw the same vision that Ms. P had described earlier—the little girl in the corner crying.

Hannah handed Ms. Priscilla back the mirror and dug into her wallet to retrieve forty-five dollars. Ms. Priscilla looked surprised after counting the money.

"It's only thirty-five dollars, dear."

"I know, Ms. P. I wanted to bless you because you're always helping me with your words of encouragement and prayers."

"Well, may God give it back to you a hundredfold."

"See, that's what I mean," Hannah stated.

"I'm just repeating the Word, sweetheart. I challenge you to start reading it again. You said your daddy and aunt kept you in church when you were younger. Well, that means you have the Word in you. Now, it's time to get back to it. Get back to him. Allow his will to be done in your life. I want you to pick a scripture every morning. It will bless your life. You young people have all those smart phones and things, so download the Bible and read it. I just use Old Faithful."

"What's Old Faithful, Ms. P?" Hannah asked, standing and brushing the trimmed hair off her shirt.

"My old, raggedy paper Bible I purchased from that Christian bookstore up the street years ago. I've had it for over ten years. It's falling apart, but I just stick the pages back in the right section and keep on reading."

"Wow. You've had the same Bible for ten years?"

"Yes, ma'am. If it ain't broke, there's no need trying to fix it."

Hannah giggled because she could have sworn Ms. Priscilla had just informed her that the pages were falling out of her Bible.

"Well, I'll see you next time. Thanks again, Ms. P for always having a listening ear. I'll continue to think about what you shared with me," Hannah said, hugging Ms. Priscilla.

"Remember, I'm always here for you, sweetheart. Drive safely."

"Yes, ma'am. See you later Ms. Angela," Hannah stated. She turned and waved at the other women under the dryers before heading out to her car. She climbed into the driver's seat and began to talk to God. *I never knew that I wanted things more than you. I only want to be a good mother. I only want Mama's love. I want to be healed. I want to forget about the abuse and all of the hurt I feel. Is that so bad?* Hannah asked. It was hard to let her guard down. *God you have disappointed me more than I can count.*

I'm not like people. Surrender it all to me. You were not equipped to carry it. At the sound of God's voice, Hannah tried to open up her heart.

She asked God for the strength to give him her pain.

The abuse.

Her mom's rejection.

The miscarriage.

The endometriosis.

The strength to trust him.

Most of all, she pleaded with God to help her open her whole heart.

To allow him to love her.

Then, she turned the ignition and headed home.

CHAPTER FOURTEEN

Thursday, April 17

It was 4:00 P.M. Hannah had arrived home from work a few minutes ago. Levi wouldn't get home until around 6:00. After changing into a pair of comfortable pajama bottoms, Hannah went into the kitchen and opened the pack of chicken she had taken out that morning before she left and placed it in a pan of water in the refrigerator.

She dumped the chicken into the sink, ran water over it, placed the pieces back into the pan and began seasoning it. She then set the oven to 350 degrees and placed the pan inside. Hannah had been craving some barbecue and sautéed vegetables, so she decided to make some. Grabbing a pan, she rinsed it and poured a small amount of coconut oil in it, then turned it on medium heat.

After cleaning up the countertop, Hannah went to the living room to retrieve her cell phone from the couch. She unlocked her phone and began to check her messages. She frowned as she noticed a message from her mom. Hannah clicked to open it.

What in the world?

I see you and your husband are still trying to manipulate Brittany into adopting her baby. I wonder why you're trying so hard. Like I told Brittany, that is crazy. What are y'all going to tell that child, her auntie is really her mama? Why are you not having your own child?

"Really?" Hannah stated out loud. "I'm so tired of this."

Hannah fumed. She wanted to reply but decided against it. She closed her messages as she grew more angry. She attempted to shake it off, determined to not let the words get to her.

Lost in thought, Hannah was reminded she was supposed to be cooking by the smell of the coconut oil on the stove. "Oh, my goodness, I'm about to burn my house down."

Hannah grabbed the vegetables she had chopped and seasoned. She placed them in the pan, although she didn't have an appetite anymore. Most of the vegetables were squash, one of her favorites. She turned it down to a simmer and went over to the island. After a few minutes of trying to calm down, and pacing back and forth, she decided to call Brittany.

"Hello," Brittany answered on the first ring.

"Hey, sis."

"What's going on?"

"I just got one of those crazy texts from Mama," Hannah said.

"What did it say?"

"She's talking about I'm manipulating you into the adoption and wanting to know why I'm not having my own kids."

"What?" Brittany screamed into the phone. "I know Mama didn't."

"Yes, she did."

"Sis, you know I haven't told Mama nothing about your condition."

"I believe you. I hope you don't think I'm trying to manipulate you or anything."

"Why would you say that? I was the one who offered to let you and Levi adopt the baby. Mama has probably been drinking again."

"She may be. I think she needs to get some help with that drinking problem," Hannah said.

"With that anger problem too," Brittany replied.

"True."

"I'm going to call her right now. She needs to stop this mess. You're my sister—her daughter—and I'm tired of her being so hateful."

"It's okay, Brit. I'll handle it. I'll give Mama a call. Let me call you back."

"Are you sure?"

"Yes," Hannah whispered.

"I'm so sorry, sis. I hate you have to go through this. Love you."

"I love you too," Hannah said before hanging up.

Hannah checked on the vegetables. She turned the stove all the way down before grabbing her phone. Her hands trembled as she dialed her mom's number.

This has to stop now.

Her heart seemed to skip a beat as she pressed the call button. Hannah's mom finally picked up on the third ring.

"Hello," her mom answered, sounding annoyed.

"*Ummm.* H–Hey, Mama," Hannah stammered.

"Hey," she said, sounding uninterested.

"This is Hannah. How are you doing?"

"I know who this is."

"Mama, this craziness has got to stop."

"You're right. This craziness with you trying to adopt your own niece when your sister is able bodied is what's crazy. Why are you so determined to adopt Brittany's baby?"

"Mama, I'm not doing this with you. This is between me, Brittany and Levi, not you."

"Like I said, why are you doing it?"

"I'm tired of this nonsense, Mama. All I've ever wanted to do was build a relationship with you. Here you go doing everything you can to try to break me again. How much more? Huh, Mama? How much more are you going to do?"

"Ain't nobody trying to break you. I've been through stuff too."

"I'm sure, but I didn't do it. Goodbye, Mama."

***

When Levi arrived home, Hannah shared with him the details of her conversation with her mom as they ate. She could tell he wasn't happy by the clenching of his jaw.

"So how was work?"

"It was okay. It was work," Levi replied.

"Did you get a chance to work in the nursery any?"

"Not much. I was so frustrated with Mama."

"Babe, I'm getting tired of the way she's treating you. I've seen your pain over the years. This has to stop. She doesn't seem to be willing to change."

"I know she's my mom, but today was it. I can't keep going through this craziness. I just want to get this adoption done."

"I know you love your mama, but you have to let go, maybe even stop communicating with her for a while and ignore what she has to say about the adoption."

"You are a true blessing to me. Thank you for walking with me through this."

"For the hundredth time, you don't need to thank me. I want you to focus on your own mental health."

"I will."

Hannah cleaned the dishes and went into the living room to wait for Levi. They were going to take a walk. Hannah walked back into the kitchen to grab her keys. As she was heading back over to the couch, Levi came bounding down the stairs.

"You ready?"

"Yes!" Hannah said, following him to the door and stepping out onto their covered porch. The sun had set, but they headed out anyway. Hannah turned to lock the door. Their neighbor, Mrs. Jenkins was pulling into her driveway. She lived in the tan-colored town home a few doors down. The woman waved as she headed inside. Hannah and Levi locked hands and started down the walkway.

"Are we still going to Mama Jefferson's next weekend?" Hannah said as they strolled.

"Yes. She wants us to go with her to the churches *Be the Light* community event she spearheaded."

"Sounds good. She is such a giver."

"Yes. Ever since I can remember, she has served those in need."

"That's a great thing."

"She has been a great role model."

"Yea, I hope Mama stops drinking and comes around someday."

"I really hope so too. I don't know why there's so much strife in families, especially parents and their children. There should be a deep connection there." Levi added.

"It should be, but that's not always the case. I know all too well from my own experience and overhearing some of my students. When we become parents, I want to break that."

"Of course."

"I mean, I want our child, adopted or not, to know that they are loved. I don't want them to ever question that," Hannah said as they turned at the stop sign.

"I agree," Levi said, squeezing her hand.

"I've felt unloved since I was very young. I always felt that Mama didn't care for me. I mean, the way she would yell at me and tell me I was like my daddy... Her tone would be harsh. Then, I went to live with Aunt Loretta and Malcolm. Aunt Loretta started off showing me love, but when I told her what Malcolm did, she changed."

"Hannah, as I've told you before, their responses were not your fault. As far as Aunt Loretta, she did what most women would do: believe her man."

"I know, but it doesn't make it easier. But I guess it's like the old saying goes *hurt people, hurt people.* They may not realize they're hurting others because they can't see passed their own hurt."

"Pretty much. But you, sweetheart, can break the cycle. You don't have to do the same thing.

"You are such an old soul, so much wisdom."

"Who are you calling old, woman?" Levi said, smiling.

"You're a sweet teddy bear."

"Okay, teddy bear. More like a lion. I'm supposed to protect you, and I hate that I can't take away your pain, but soon our house will be filled with joy when little Neveah gets here."

"Yeah, I can't wait to hold her," Hannah finally said, locking arms as they admired the stars before turning back toward home.

CHAPTER FIFTEEN

Friday, April 18

It was the last day of spring break for Hannah. Her eyes popped open at the sound of her phone's alarm. She wanted to get some things done in the nursery today before returning to work on Monday. She and Levi had thought about doing a baby shower, more like the small celebration at Applebee's, but they changed their minds and decided to send out a baby registry instead to a few close relatives and friends.

She lay there for a few minutes then stretched and leaned over to kiss Levi on the cheek. He didn't stir. She let him sleep because he had to be up in the next few minutes to not be late for work. He had been exhausted from doing double duty at Clayton County Utilities and Water. Hannah now understood why they got so many complaints. *They need to stop being cheap and hire more people.*

Hannah lay her head back on their brown leather headboard for a few moments. Feeling more hopeful, Hannah still hung on to Ms. Priscilla's encouraging words. She wanted to get back to reading the Bible and prayer. She wanted to learn to trust God with her life. She had hoped for her relationship to change with her mom but no such luck. Now, she planned to take Ms. P's advice and give it to God. Grabbing her cell phone off the nightstand, she rolled out of bed and went down to the kitchen to make a cup of coffee. It was only 6:15, so she had some time before she planned to get her to-do list done.

She pulled opened the drawer that housed a variety of coffees, teas and even hot chocolate for Levi. She grabbed her mug from the cabinet above the stove, rinsed it out and selected the Folgers dark roast. Still a little groggy, Hannah needed a pick-me-up. She placed her mug beneath the Keurig and grabbed the hazelnut creamer from the fridge. After adding a generous amount to her coffee, as well as a few natural sweet drops, she sat at the island to savor the moment of silence.

Hannah bowed her head and began to pray. *Dear God, I want to continue to open up to you. I've had so many disappointments with Mama and then with losing the baby and the diagnosis. I guess I started seeing you as Mama and Aunt Loretta. I felt that you had disappointed me too. Then, came the pain of our loss. I became angry. I'm sorry. I don't know where to start. I know your word says that you love us with an everlasting love. I struggle with that. Why do you love me? Mama hates me, but I've always loved her. I've never stopped. Why can't you change her heart? Why did I miscarry and have to deal with these treatments? Thank you for touching Brittany's heart and her asking us to adopt the baby. I'm looking forward to being a mom now. I want to be a better mother. It was hard not having Mama, and it's hard to let go of still wanting her in my life. I want to share things with her, Lord. I want to spend time getting to know her. Is that so bad? It hurts. I really want to allow you to love me. Please help me to trust you more and more. In Jesus' name. Amen.*

After her prayer, Hannah sat in silence for a few moments. As she sat there, she heard, *The love you need is in me.* She knew it was God speaking to her again. She welcomed his words. Her heart warmed over as she whispered, "Help me not to reject your voice anymore." Not knowing what else to say and trying to let down the rest of the wall she had built around her heart, Hannah just sat there with her eyes closed. She knew God had gotten passed the small opening because of the peace she felt at that moment. She sighed and sat quiet a little longer. Hannah then unlocked her phone and opened the Bible app she had downloaded last night. As she waited, she took a sip of her coffee. "Ugh, it's cold." Hannah stood to reheat it in the microwave. Coming back over to the island, she began reading day one of a Bible plan she found by Pastor Tony Evans. Hannah was intrigued by the title *Bouncing Back from Disappointment.* Her heart raced as she read one of the scriptures for the first day, "But seek first His kingdom and His righteousness, and all these things will be added to you." Hannah's eyes filled with tears as she finished verse thirty-three of Matthew.

She then read the next set of scriptures listed. Not yet ready to read the devotional, she previewed the list of scriptures for day two and clicked on Psalm 34:18. She shivered, remembering those words. Her youth mentor, Ms. Silvers, had read them to her all those years ago, and now God was reminding her that he is near to the brokenhearted. Hannah said a silent prayer, thanking God once again for being with her.

After finishing her coffee and nearing the end of the first devotional, Hannah read the next one and began to search for similar scriptures online as she heard Levi moving around, getting ready to leave for work. He came rushing into the kitchen, grabbed his lunch from the fridge, and gave her a long, lingering kiss, "I love you," he said before dashing through the door and into the garage.

"I love you too," Hannah yelled through the closed door.

Before she knew it, she had gone in the office to retrieve a notebook. For the first time in years, she began to journal. She wrote what she had learned about God and how he helped others bounce back from disappointments. Hannah wrote and wrote until she had written out three pages. She then found herself writing a short poem. Her heart was full. She said a prayer for her mom.

Closing her notebook, Hannah decided she would attend church on Sunday. She wanted to grow a relationship with God again. She would mention it to Levi. She knew he would be game. Hannah decided to invite her dad out since she hadn't seen him in a few weeks. She checked the clock. *It's 7:30 now. Daddy should be up getting ready.*

"Good morning, Daddy."

"Good morning, baby girl. What's up?"

"I figured you would be up getting ready to go in to work."

"I am."

"That's good. I wanted to ask if you would attend Ms. P's church with me and Levi on Sunday. Maybe we could grab lunch afterward."

"Sounds good, but I promised Melissa I would attend service with her and Joseph."

"Oh, okay," Hannah said, disappointed.

"Let's try for next Sunday."

"Sounds good," Hannah said.

"Looking forward to it."

"Thank you for taking care of me and being such a great dad. I've never really talked about how much my life was impacted by Mama not being there and how I pulled away from God."

"You didn't have to tell me. I could see it. Aunt Melissa, Uncle Joseph and I have been praying for you."

"Thanks, Daddy. I prayed this morning and started one of those Bible studies by Pastor Tony Evans. I even started back journaling."

"That's great. I'm so glad to hear that. And where did you find the Bible study?"

"It is in this Bible app I downloaded."

"Oh, you have to share that with me."

"I'll text the app name to you."

"Okay. And by the way, it was my job to be there for you. That's what God expected of me."

"That's what I mean, Daddy. Some men run from their responsibilities, but you didn't. Even with the drama with Mama, and even when you didn't have your own place, you asked Uncle Joseph if I could come and live with you all. I'm grateful."

"You're welcome, baby girl. I'll always be here, as long as God allows it."

"I know you don't go to church often, but you've always taught me the Bible and what God expects of us. What kept you from attending or joining a church?"

"Honestly, I never made it a priority. I work a lot on the weekends and try to get as much rest as I can. I get there as much as I can now. I accepted Christ some time ago, but I'm no angel by any stretch of the imagination."

"None of us are."

"I'm trying to be a better person every day as the Lord leads."

"I want to do the same."

"It will come. Keep crying out to the Lord. Alright, I'll check in on you later."

"Okay, Daddy."

After disconnecting, Hannah went up to the office to return her notebook. Thinking about journaling more, she opened the closet door and pulled out her box of journals. Journaling had surely given her a peace of mind during her younger years. She hadn't written in one since college.

Hannah lifted a teal one from the box after sitting it on the chair behind her. She read the front, "Don't give up. Success is just ahead." Hannah rubbed her hand across the leather material. She had found it in the Clayton State's bookstore where she first locked eyes with Levi. She would never forget that beautiful fall day. Hannah remembered it like it was yesterday. She was headed to her children's literature class and decided to run into the bookstore for some supplies. Levi had been standing over near the college paraphernalia wearing a pair of jeans and a navy Clayton State t-shirt. Hannah would never forget how handsome he looked as he stood there. She wondered why she hadn't seen him her first year on campus. He shared that he had enrolled after taking a year off.

Because she lived an hour away from campus, Hannah decided to stay in the dorms after her freshman year. Levi lived near the campus, so he stayed at home while attending school. They talked and hung out day in and day out and had been inseparable ever since.

As Hannah flipped through the journal, she smiled at the memories. She had recorded her dates with Levi. Flipping a few more pages, Hannah began reading a short children's story she had written while in college. She covered her mouth to silence her outburst of laughter. She couldn't believe how amateur her story sounded. Becoming a writer was something she always wanted to do but never got around to looking into because of life's drama. *Maybe I'll write a children's book someday,* Hannah thought, dropping the journal back inside the box and placing everything back into the closet before heading down the hall to her room. She searched her closet for an outfit for church. Settling on her teal short-sleeve, loose-fitting Maxi dress, she pulled it out and hung it on the hook behind their closet door and headed back into the office/nursery and continued painting and setting up for their new arrival. They would pick up the crib next week. Hannah was glad she chose the peach color. It was beautiful. *I didn't think this would happen for me. So grateful.*

***

Later that afternoon, Hannah prepped her hair for her date with Levi. They were attending a paint, poetry and grub event at Ms. Pearl's, a soul food restaurant about twenty minutes from their house. She set the front with rods and pinned up the back. Levi loved when her hair hung in spirals around her face, highlighting her beauty, as he described.

Hannah loved her mocha complexion. As she stared at her reflection, she was reminded of her middle school days and the one hateful classmate who called her "blacky." *Dang, that was a long time ago. I still remember that.* It had taken her some time to get over that one word. Levi would always compliment her on her beautiful skin tone, and her dad would often mention seeing his mother and the true beauty she was when he looked at her. Levi would say how much he loved his little chocolate drop. All of those positive affirmations seemed to help Hannah see the beauty that stared back at her now in the bathroom mirror. As she grew into adulthood, she began to accept herself more and more, and as a teacher, she never allowed bullying in her classroom.

After adding the final curl rod, Hannah headed downstairs to get her daily dose of Lifetime Movie Network. This past week, Hannah had watched her share of crazy wives and psycho husbands. She had to admit she loved it. She understood why it was called Television for Women.

After sitting for two hours watching yet another drama, Hannah clicked off the television and went to her massive bookshelf in the office. She had collected many titles over the years with various authors and genres. She considered reading one of them over but decided to take a nap before her date instead.

As she headed down the stairs to stretch out on the couch, the doorbell chimed. Hannah wondered who that could be. She wasn't expecting anyone. She headed to her bedroom to throw on a t-shirt over her tank top and thick pajama bottoms. Hearing the doorbell again, she hurried downstairs. As she neared the door, she saw Ms. Priscilla standing there.

Ms. P? Hannah opened the door with a surprised expression. "Well, hey, Ms. P. How are you?"

"I'm good, sweetheart. I just came by to check on you."

"You didn't have to do that, Ms. Priscilla. I'm doing okay," Hannah said, trying to figure out how Ms. P got her address, then she remembered the time a while back when she came by to pray with them after they'd purchased their townhome.

"Well, let me see for myself. Are you going to make me stand out here all day, missy?" Ms. Priscilla asked with a smirk.

"Oh, no. Come on in."

"Thank you, sweetness," Ms. Priscilla stated as they walked into the living room.

"So, what's up, Ms. P. Have a seat," Hannah offered, pointing to the center of the sectional. "How are things at the shop?"

"They're great, to God be the glory! You two have really fixed this place up. I love the cozy feeling."

"Thank you! We love it too. You probably remember how we went back and forth, trying to decide if we should purchase a single-family home or not. Levi loves that there's not a lot of yard—less mowing for him."

"I understand. That works. And you still have space for a little one," Ms. Priscilla added. Hannah smiled.

"Yes. Our little one will be here soon."

"Dear, I'm not talking about your sister's baby. I'm talking about the miracle that God wants to perform in your life."

"Ms. P, you remember I told you about the endometriosis, right?" Hannah said softly.

"I know what man said, but God can do anything but fail."

"That would be great," Hannah replied. She didn't have anything else. She wanted to get that level of faith. She had opted to believe that the adoption was the miracle she was receiving.

"How are you?" Ms. Priscilla asked, eyeing Hannah.

"I'm good."

"How are you feeling, really? Emotionally? Have you been reading the Word like I suggested? You've been on my heart."

"I actually started this morning. I prayed and began to journal like I used to do when I was younger."

"That's good. Keep at it. You'll experience healing, a change in your heart, and a change in those you pray for too."

"I plan to."

"Sweetheart, remember that God's very essence is love."

"I know. That's what Aunt Melissa and Daddy taught me, but I have to admit again, it's hard for me to understand."

"As I said, you've been on my heart. I've been praying for you. It will all work together for your good."

Hannah thought she had misheard Ms. P. She was trying to process what she had just heard. *How can so much pain work for my good?* Hannah just didn't understand that statement. She had great respect for Ms. Priscilla, so she decided to hear her out.

"You okay?" Ms. Priscilla asked, with a worried expression. Hannah sat with her head bowed, rubbing her hands together. She finally spoke.

"Ms. P., I don't understand statements like that. I mean, how can all of my pain be working together for my good?"

"That's not what I meant. I mean that God can use it to get you where he's calling you to be. He's calling you to him, Hannah."

"I really do want to continue to let down my guard and trust him, Ms. P."

"Sweetheart, we go through things in this life, things that are unfair and often very painful. However, God's love for us never changes. He wants to heal you, Hannah. Where you feel empty, God wants to fill those barren places. You see, a diagnosis may have you believing that you can't have children, but it's not bigger than God. I'm speaking by faith of what God is showing me. He's the one who opens wombs and heals, but he wants to heal the inner man first."

Hannah pondered on Ms. P's words. She needed to understand what God wanted for her.

"Thank you, Ms. P, I feel comfortable talking to you."

"Well, thank you, sweetness."

"I have a question. I don't want to offend you."

"Baby, you aren't going to offend me. I'm here to do God's work."

Hannah hesitated for a moment before speaking, "Why does God want to use me?" Hannah asked.

"Sweetheart, we can't truly know God unless we've had to walk through something, and once he's brought us through, he wants to use us to help bring others through as well. People rejected and abused you, maybe because they were abused or rejected or because they're simply allowing Satan to use them. God hasn't rejected you, nor is he an abuser. Unfortunately, we live in a fallen world where sin and evil exist. If God takes control, he also must take total control of you and me as well. That would mean that you no longer have a free will. He wouldn't violate his own law. We wouldn't be able to choose him for ourselves any longer if he did, so he uses us to reach others and help lead them to him. They then get to choose him for themselves as well."

"Wow, Ms. P. I never thought about it that way."

"All credit belongs to the Holy Spirit. He's speaking."

"I look at you, Ms. P, and I see something different. I see your heart of love for God and people."

"Again, all the glory belongs to God."

"I hope to get to where you are someday—I mean your relationship with God."

"I know what you meant, and you will because you desire to. That's the first step. We can't heal ourselves. We try, but it never works because we go about it the wrong way."

"What do you mean by that?"

"God is calling us to relationship, one where we walk in communion with Christ. That takes a surrendering of our hearts. If we're trying to be our own god, we never get to that place. Our relationship with God is the key thing that will set us free. Religion is just following the rules, regulations and keeping traditions. That's how you can see people go to church but not change. God wants to do an inner work."

"Thank you for explaining that to me. I want to know more."

"Just remember, God is the eternal creator. Love and acceptance flow from him. If we can't trust the creator, then who can we trust? Come join us again on Sunday. I've missed you. I also lead the women's group there, and many of the women have experienced some form of trauma. We'll start our new small groups on Wednesday evenings at 7:30. I think you'll enjoy it and learn so much."

"I was already planning to attend," Hannah replied.

"Well, all right then. No pressure. I promise."

"Thanks for coming to check up on me, Ms. P. I'm going to try to take me a nap before my date with Levi later."

"Oh, that's so nice. That's a great thing. Spend as much time as you can together. Don't let go of each other in this time. I wish I could have spent more time with my Theodore. He worked two jobs trying to take care of us. He would be exhausted when he finally had a day off. Now that he's gone and our two are grown, I spend my time pouring into others. I did start scheduling time once a month with my son and daughter."

"That's great, Ms. P. I'll definitely take that advice."

"Well, I'm going to run on and let you get your rest. I pray to see you Sunday or the Wednesday after next."

"I'll be there Sunday."

"I'm so glad to hear that. Love you, sweetness," Ms. Priscilla stated, rising to hug Hannah.

"Love you too."

"Alright. Let me get on out of here."

"Okay. Have a good rest of your day," Hannah stated, walking Ms. Priscilla to the door. She waited until she got into her car before closing the front door.

She then grabbed a throw from the hall closet and headed back over to the couch. Hannah grabbed her phone to set her timer to alert her in an hour. She then lifted her feet onto the couch, positioned her decorative pillow under her head and drifted off to sleep.

CHAPTER SIXTEEN

Monday, April 28

The school day had ended. Hannah grabbed her bags and headed out to her car, waving at the other third-grade teachers as they sat at their desks still working. Most of the time, Hannah kept to herself. She didn't talk much to the other teachers outside of Robin and Anton. Hannah didn't feel much of a connection with them. She was glad to have her class all day. She wasn't sure what she would do if she had to deal with switching classes and hearing some of their complaining.

Hannah was on her way to meet Brittany for one of her scheduled prenatal doctor's appointments. Her sister was thirty-three weeks now. Hannah had suggested she start going to Dr. Sarin in her first trimester. She and Levi had been helping to pay for her prenatal vitamins and her co-pays. Brittany was still on their mom's insurance, thankfully. Their mom had threatened to take her off so many times Hannah lost count. On her way to Dr. Sarin's, she decided to call Uncle Joseph. Her dad told her he wasn't feeling well.

"Hey, Unc," Hannah sang.

"How are you, sweetheart?"

"I'm doing okay. Just leaving work and headed to meet Brittany at her doctor's appointment."

"How is she feeling?"

"She's been okay. She said she's been pretty tired, trying to push through her full load of classes."

"I bet. Well, we've been praying for you all."

"Thanks. So, how are you feeling?"

"I'm doing okay. I felt like I was coming down with something."

"Auntie told me. You make sure you get you some rest."

"I'm trying. Your aunt done broke out the old remedies, so I'm feeling a little better now.

"That's good to hear. What did she give you, tea, lemon and honey? Ginger?"

"I little bit of all of that." Uncle Joseph laughed, followed by a light cough.

"How about Levi and I come out to Norcross on Saturday. I know we haven't been able to get out there much. We probably won't have a lot of time once the baby comes, at least until she gets a little older. Maybe we can bring you and Auntie some food."

"You don't have to do that. I might feel well enough to throw together a li'l chicken bone or two."

"Now, you know I love your barbeque, but you don't have to do that. I just want to see you."

"Well, if I'm feeling up to it, I will definitely put together a little something," Uncle Joseph joked.

"Well, I'll see you then."

"You know you're always welcome here. This will always be your home."

"I know. Alright. Tell Auntie I said hello."

"I will. She's yelling at you from the kitchen."

"Hey, Auntie," Hannah said.

"Alright. I'm looking forward to seeing you."

"Me too. Have you been watching your diet?" Hannah asked.

"You know your aunt watches me like a hawk, so I don't have a choice. She makes sure I monitor my blood sugar and blood pressure."

"That's good to hear. I'm trying to eat better now too. I was reading about how changing up your diet can help reduce endometriosis pain and growth."

"That's good. You take care of yourself and tell Brittany hello for us."

"I will. Love you and Auntie," Hannah said, hanging up and pulling into the doctor's office parking lot.

When she walked in, Brittany was browsing through an *Essence* magazine. Hannah walked over and took a seat next to her. Hannah couldn't believe how fast time had flown. *The baby will be here in no time. Gotta finish setting everything together.*

"Hey, sis," Brittany said.

"What's up? How long have you been waiting?" Hannah asked, looking up at the clock. Brittany's appointment was at 3:30.

"Just a few minutes."

"Oh, okay. Uncle Joseph said hello."

"Okay. How's he doing?"

"He's not feeling well, but he said he's getting better with Auntie's old remedies. We are going to go out and see him on Saturday.

"Okay, I hope he feels better."

"You want to come with us? I'm sure Uncle Joseph and Auntie won't mind."

"I would love to, but I've got another paper due on Monday, so I've gotta stay and work on it,"

Brittany said, avoiding eye contact with Hannah. *I wonder what that's about. Maybe she's just a ball of nerves.*

"Girl, I don't miss that school stuff. I want to get my master's, but I'm not up to writing papers. I love writing, but not all of that technical gibberish."

"You should get your master's. What do you think you'd want to get it in?"

"Education, definitely. Maybe leadership."

"That's what's up. So, are you thinking about looking into being a principal or something one day?"

"Oh, I don't know about that. They have too much on their plate."

"Maybe a teacher leader or something. Or help with student discipline, maybe."

"Brittany Hamilton," Nurse Maggie called out from the open doorway.

Hannah waved at her. She was glad her sister was being seen by those she was familiar with. It brought her comfort.

Hannah and Brittany stood and headed to the back. Nurse Maggie asked Hannah how she'd been.

"I've been doing okay. Just trying to deal with this endometriosis."

"I'm sure. So many women are being diagnosed with it. I know there are more studies being done to see how best to treat it."

"I hope they develop something that doesn't cause a lot of side effects."

"I agree. Which one are you on?"

"The Progestin-only pills. I had to be switched from the estrogen and progestin combination because I was experiencing some side effects."

"Well, it sounds like the specialist is monitoring properly. Unfortunately, they all have some kind of side effect."

After chatting with Nurse Maggie for another minute, she instructed Hannah to wait in the area just outside of the room until she got Brittany's weight and took her vitals. Hannah checked her Instagram while she waited. She followed a journaling hashtag. She had been thinking about getting back into journaling but being more creative with them. She followed another hashtag she found interesting. Hannah was so engaged in viewing the awesome journals until she didn't hear the nurse talking to her.

"Oh, I'm sorry."

"Come with me," Nurse Maggie said, leading them a few rooms down. Hannah took a seat in the chair by the door. The nurse instructed Brittany to change into a gown and take a seat on the exam table. She informed Brittany that she and the doctor would return in a few moments.

"Are you nervous?" Hannah asked, taking a seat in the chair by the door.

"A little."

"You're almost at the finish line. It's going to be okay," Hannah said.

"I know. I'm just a little more nervous than usual since the birth is so close now," Brittany stated.

"It's going to be fine. I'm here for you every step of the way."

"Hannah, I don't want the baby to be angry with me when she gets older."

"Stop worrying about that, sis. We'll work through that," Hannah said. She was also nervous.

"Knock, knock," Dr. Sarin said, entering the room with Nurse Mattie behind her. Brittany climbed up on the bed. "How are you doing, young lady?"

"I'm fine," Brittany said.

"That's good to hear. And how are you, my dear?" she asked, turning toward Hannah.

"I'm really excited. Levi and I are adopting my sister's baby."

"Well, that's wonderful news, dear," Dr. Sarin replied. Once again, Hannah noticed Brittany's pained expression as Dr. Sarin turned to congratulate Brittany for her bravery of being able to give the child a good life with family.

"Thanks," her sister said, without emotion.

While she waited for them to begin, Hannah opened her Pinterest app again. She searched for journal ideas and baby items. She pinned books she planned to buy, toys, types of bottles, and more. Hannah then searched for a stroller. It was almost summer break. She planned to get out more and enjoy time with Levi and their new baby.

"You can come over now," the nurse said, startling Hannah. As she stood on the right side of the bed, she saw the fear in Brittany's eyes. She moved closer as the nurse squeezed the gel on Brittany's belly while Dr. Sarin placed on her gloves. Hannah held her sister's hand and smiled at her.

"Try to relax."

"I'm trying."

Hannah watched how Brittany's eyes lit up as she watched the machine. Her sister smiled as the baby kicked more, seeming to want to be left alone. Dr. Sarin asked if they had thought of a name.

"Yes," Hannah said.

"What are you planning to call this little precious angel?"

"Neveah," Hannah blurted out without hesitation.

"Oh, my goodness. That's a beautiful name," Dr. Sarin said.

Brittany remained silent as she stared at the monitor. Hannah began clapping and cheering. Streams of tears rolled down Brittany's cheeks as she seemed unable to take her eyes off the screen.

"Congratulations. You have a healthy little girl here," Dr. Sarin said.

"Thank you," Hannah said. Brittany was still quiet.

Dr. Sarin instructed Brittany to get dressed, and they could pick up the sonogram pictures on the way out. Hannah stepped into the hall, allowing her sister to have a moment to herself. Hannah's heart broke for her sister. She was sure this wasn't easy, but this was Brittany's decision. It was far better than taking the baby's life. Hannah would help Brittany through this. That's the least she could do for her sister giving them such a precious gift. She would be forever indebted to Brittany.

A few minutes later, Brittany exited the room, tears still streaming. It seemed to take all of her energy to say, "Can I talk to you outside?"

"Sure. Do you have to stop at the desk?" Hannah asked.

"Yes, just to drop off this paper," Brittany replied as if every word pained her.

"I'll walk with you."

As they walked, Hannah imagined what her sister wanted to talk about. Had their mom sent her another message that she didn't mention? Had Travis said something else crazy to her? Whatever it was, it had taken a toll on Brittany.

They exited the building and went to sit in Hannah's car. She didn't want people to see her sister like this.

"So, what did you want to talk about?" Hannah asked.

"I'm sorry, Hannah," Brittany said between more tears.

"Sorry for what, Brit? I told you we all make mistakes. I'm not perfect either."

"It's not that," Brittany mumbled.

"Then what is it?"

"I can't... I just can't..." Brittany cried.

"You can't what, Brit? You're scaring me. What's going on?"

"I–I...can't give up the baby."

"What?" Hannah said, her heartrate speeding up.

"I can't give her up."

"Brittany, I don't understand. We are due to adopt the baby not long from now."

"I know. After all of those messages from Ma..."

At those words, Hannah lost it on her sister. "Is that what this is about—that craziness from Mama? So, she got you to change your mind?"

"No, it's n—"

"You know what, save it. I don't want to hear it, Brittany. You brought this to me. I didn't ask you. You brought it to *me*," Hannah screamed. "Now, after all of these months of preparation and getting my hopes up, you come with this. How do you plan to raise this baby? Your trifling boyfriend sure isn't planning to help you." Hannah fumed. She couldn't believe this.

"Why are you being so mean? That's not even you."

"Did you just ask me that? I have the right to be angry right now. Did you think about how I would feel about all of this? No! Yes, I'm angry."

"You know what? You're no different from Mama. You could care less about me right now because you want what you want," Brittany spewed.

"You did not just compare me to Mama's hateful ways. I am nothing like that. Never will be. Why don't you just get out of my car and go figure out how you're going to take care of yourself and a baby."

"How could you say that to me right now?" Brittany cried. "In the moment that I need you the most, you are more concerned about yourself."

"Whatever," Hannah stated, looking out of the front windshield.

"You know what, fine. You don't have to worry about me calling you when I give birth because I'd rather have this baby alone then have your hateful self anywhere near me," Brittany finally said before opening the door, standing, and slamming Hannah's car door, causing the whole car to shake.

CHAPTER SEVENTEEN

Monday, April 28

Hannah hadn't drank alcohol since college. And even then, she'd only done it because it seemed to be the thing to do, but she eventually decided against it as she thought about her mom. Hannah had watched what it had done to her, and she didn't want to ruin her life. She had been a pretty responsible adult thus far, but at that moment, she needed to feel numb. She couldn't believe how much had happened in just a short time. After sitting in the parking lot of the doctor's office for over an hour, replaying what had just happened between her and Brittany, Hannah finally pulled out onto Main Street.

I lost my child. Told I can't possibly have anymore. Mama hates me. The stress of the treatments for endometriosis. Now this. I may not ever have the opportunity to be a mother. This is too much! I just don't care anymore. How could Brittany do this to me?

Hannah took Old Dixie Road to I-285 and drove a few exits passed her own. She made a right off the highway and pulled into the parking lot of Liberty Package Store. After requesting a brown paper bag and cup for her Seagram's Gin, she remembered she needed a can of Coca-Cola. She left the bag on the counter and walked over to the refrigerator to retrieve her chaser. Hannah wanted all the pain to go away, and she figured this would do it.

After checking for anyone she knew, Hannah jumped into her car and drove a little further. She pulled over into a wooded park. Hannah drove all the way to the other side, surrounded by trees. She turned off the engine. She opened the bottle and poured a cup, adding the soda. Hannah swallowed it in two gulps then decided to call her mom and give her a piece of her mind. She pulled her cell phone from her purse and searched her contact log for her mom's number since it had been a while since she'd spoken to her. Hannah felt as bold as a lion now. She was tired of the mistreatment. She was angry, and she wanted her to know it. She pressed on Mama and waited for her to answer. Her mom picked up on the second ring.

"Hello."

"Are you happy now?"

"What?" Hannah's mom asked, sounding confused.

"I said, are you happy now," Hannah screamed into the phone.

"I don't know who you think you are talking to like that."

"I'm talking to you, Mama, the woman who has mistreated me all of my life. The woman who has held a grudge against me because she messed around on her husband. The woman who would rather her younger daughter suffer and possibly have to drop out of college than to see me be happy raising that baby. I'm talking to you."

"Girl, you better check yourself when you're talking to me. I said what I said. That adoption was foolish talk."

"It wasn't foolish talk. I, Brittany's sister, was willing and able to adopt the baby and allow her to finish school."

"And I'm just supposed to believe that you and your husband are these perfect citizens. Just wanted to help her, huh?"

"Mama, Brittany asked us for help. What are you willing to do for your own daughter?"

"She got that baby. Now, she needs to be a woman and take care of her, not you. And I ask again, why are you so angry right now, huh?"

"Why do you hate me so much?"

"I don't hate you, and you know it."

"Mama, how can I know that? You haven't shown it at all," Hannah said.

"And why are you calling me and not Mr. Perfect?"

"Daddy doesn't have anything to do with this. This is between me and you. I'm sick of this. All I ever wanted was for you to love me—for you to accept me. I'm your daughter. I lost my own child, which you didn't even know about because you haven't wanted to talk to me other than to be hateful. Mama, I have endometriosis, a condition that causes infertility, but you could care less. You only care about yourself," Hannah finally said before hanging up.

Hannah then beat her hands on the steering wheel and wailed, "Why me, God? Why me? What did I do so bad?"

After weeping for several more minutes, Hannah finally wiped away her tears and poured another cup of alcohol. Hannah didn't stop drinking until all of the half-pint bottle was gone. She suddenly felt dizzy and leaned her head back on the driver's seat. Becoming drowsy, she closed her eyes and fell asleep.

***

Hannah opened her eyes and looked around. It was pitch black outside. *What in the world? My head is throbbing.*

She sat up and noticed she was inside her car. Hannah eyed the empty liquor bottle on the passenger seat and gazed out through her windshield. Suddenly, everything came rushing back to her: the argument with Brittany. The liquor store. The drive to the park. The conversation with her mom.

Dang, what time is it? Hannah wondered, lifting her phone. *Ten o'clock. Oh, no!* Hannah's eyes widened. *Levi is probably worried.*

Hannah placed her phone back down, straightened herself in the driver's seat and turned the ignition. Before pulling off, her phone beeped several times. She lifted it again. There were missed calls and messages from Levi and her dad. Hannah clicked to read Levi's first.

Hannah's heart ached as she read her husband's series of messages.

Hannah, where are you?

Brittany came by and told me what happened.

Hannah, why aren't you picking up?

Babe, you have to talk to me. I'm getting worried. We can still believe God for a little one.

Hannah, answer the phone. Please tell me you're safe.

After reading all ten of Levi's messages, Hannah pulled out of the parking lot. As she drove, she regretted sinking, once again, to the poison that had consumed her mom all these years. She felt worse now than before she took the first sip of that bottle of gin. Hannah had no clue as to what she would say to her husband, so she didn't bother to call. *I've got to find some mouthwash or something.*

Before getting on the expressway, Hannah stopped at the convenience store just before the exit. She ran in and purchased a travel-sized bottle of mouthwash. She opened it and poured some of the liquid into the top and swished it around in her mouth several times and spit it out on the ground.

Hannah then grabbed the liquor bottle, cup, soda can and brown paper bag and dumped the contents into the trash can just outside the store.

As she drove home, she found herself swerving a little, Hannah prayed Levi wouldn't be able to tell she had been drinking. Moments later, her phone rang. She looked down to check it. It was Levi. Before Hannah answered, she took a deep breath.

"Hello."

"Babe, where in the world are you?"

"I'm on my way."

"Where have you been all day?"

"I went to the park not far from us."

"Really, and you didn't think you should call me and tell me? I've been worried."

"I'm sorry, Levi," Hannah stated, trying to keep the car steady. The blast of someone's horn made her aware she had drifted in the other lane.

"Hannah, is everything okay?"

"I'm okay."

"You don't sound okay."

"I'm fine."

"How far away are you?"

"About two exits."

"Okay. I'll wait until you get here to continue this conversation."

"Okay," Hannah finally said before disconnecting the line. She wasn't in the mood to talk to Levi about what had happened. She was done. *I tried. I don't know how much more my heart can take. I might as well get used to the new normal. No mama. No child. Maybe it's just not meant to be,* Hannah thought as she neared the exit toward home.

After arriving home, Hannah prayed Levi wouldn't be angry with her. No such luck. As soon as she unlocked the garage door, he came bounding down the stairs. She took her time entering and closing the door. Hannah passed Levi without a word as she headed up to their bedroom. She just didn't have the strength to hold a conversation.

"Ah, babe. What's going on?" Levi inquired, following her up the stairs.

"Nothing, Levi. I don't feel like talking right now," Hannah said, standing at the top of the stairs looking passed him.

"Brittany told me she changed her mind. She apologized. I'm sorry. I know this hurts you. It hurts me too, but we have to talk about this."

"I don't care anymore."

"Hannah, don't say that."

"I don't."

"I hate to see you like this," Levi stated, walking up the stairs to hug her. She stiffened as he stood there for a moment. Hannah looked up at him, noticing the frown on his face.

"*Ummm,* babe, why are you acting so weird?"

"Acting weird how?"

"You aren't yourself. Wait a minute. Have you been drinking?" he questioned. Hannah pulled away and walked into the bedroom, pulling out her pajamas.

"No. What are you talking about?"

"Hannah, have you been drinking and driving?"

"Levi, leave me alone."

"Why are you avoiding me? Tell me what's going on with you."

"Nothing," Hannah said, throwing the clothes she was holding across the room. "Nothing is going on with me. I lost my baby. I'm struggling getting pregnant, and today my sister changes her mind after all of these months. Do you know how much that hurts?"

"Babe, we have each other."

"What does that matter if I can't be a mother too?" Hannah spewed. Regretting every word, she looked up at Levi to apologize. She could see the pain in his eyes. He stood silently before speaking.

"Babe, I think we may need to look into counseling."

"Really, Levi? You're talking to me about counseling right now."

"Yes. I think it would be good."

"Well, I'm not interested in counseling."

"Hannah, it won't hurt. Here you are drinking and driving. Do you know how dangerous that is? What if something would have happened to you?"

"Levi, I'm not a kid. I can handle a few drinks. And if something would have happened to me, I wouldn't feel so much pain anymore."

"When did you start back drinking? We haven't drank since college."

"I didn't start back. I just thought it would help. Of course, it didn't. Now, I feel even more horrible."

"Babe, what about me? I'm right here. We are in this together."

"Can you just leave me alone?"

"I can't. I love you. I want you to talk to me."

"I told you I just had a few drinks. Now, I'm going to take a shower," Hannah said, walking passed him, picking up her clothes and entering the bathroom. Levi was on her heels.

"Babe, I wasn't talking about the drinking. I want you to talk to me. We can get through this together."

"I don't want to talk anymore right now," Hannah said, attempting to close the bathroom door. Levi didn't move at first. Then, he stepped back into the bedroom, and Hannah closed the door. Hannah waited before turning on the shower. She could hear Levi in the bedroom, but he soon walked down the stairs without another word.

Hannah then turned on the shower and waited for it to heat up. As she viewed her reflection in the mirror, she could see that little lost girl, her twelve-year-old self. The girl who longed to be accepted by her mother. The girl who was blamed for being too fast. She gazed at that innocent little girl and wept because she wanted to have the opportunity to love a little girl of her own and make her understand she was loved and would always be kept safe.

When Hannah came out of the bathroom, she noticed that Levi wasn't in bed. She listened for him downstairs. The house was completely silent. She assumed he was asleep on the couch. That was even better. She wasn't up to talking. She tiptoed down the stairs to get a bottle of water to take an ibuprofen. As Hannah got closer to the couch, she noticed that Levi wasn't there. *Okay, where is he?*

After grabbing a water bottle, Hannah went to check the office. She froze in front of the door. *I forgot about this room. The nursery.* They had been working on it. Hannah teared up as she opened the door. No Levi. She then walked into the guest room to see if he was there. No Levi. Hannah's heart skipped a beat. *Where is he?*

She walked back into their bedroom to retrieve her phone. As she clicked it open to call him, she noticed a recent message from him.

Babe, I'm headed to Mama's. I want to take away all of your pain, but I can't. I hurt too. I wanted that adoption as well as you. I wanted our child. I want you to know that we can make it through this together. Your words tonight sliced deep. I would never say something like that to you. Why didn't you just call me instead of putting your life in danger by drinking and driving? Did you ever stop to think how I would feel if something had happened to you? I love you more than anything, Hannah. I just need a moment.

"Really, Levi. You walk out on me because of a few words. You need a moment, but I can't take one. What happened to our vows?" Hannah cried, sinking to the floor in the fetal position.

CHAPTER EIGHTEEN

Wednesday, April 30

Hannah felt defeated. Levi was still at Mama Jefferson's. He had called and tried to talk to her, but she was so angry she didn't want to hear anything he had to say. Hannah had to admit she was even scaring herself. This was not her. She really missed him. Why was she being this way? The pain in her heart was turning her into a person she didn't want to be. She had even held out a small amount of hope that Brittany would change her mind, but why would she? Hannah replayed the hateful words to her sister in her mind. She couldn't believe it. How could she say such things to her? Brittany had apologized profusely, but Hannah didn't care. Again, she felt another precious gift had been snatched away from her. Hannah now wished she could take back all she had said.

Hannah had cried herself to sleep for the past two nights. Her hopes had been shattered, and she felt horribly guilty to be thinking of herself and not her sister. Hannah was grateful they were close to summer break. She needed it. At the moment, she was grateful for their recess break. She had planned to stay out a little longer. Her students had behaved well enough last week and so far this week. She stood on the sidewalk as they ran around and played. Most of the girls were on the swings, and the boys were playing tag or were on the monkey bars. Lesley ran over to tell her that the girls would share the swings with her. Not in the mood for one of Lesley's tantrums, Hannah shooed her away, instructing her to go play on the monkey bars, which were empty at the moment.

Hannah daydreamed about her life being different. She pictured her and Levi with two beautiful children, a boy and a girl. She pictured herself wobbling up the sidewalk to the school and up and down the stairs at home. Hannah envisioned them finishing up the nursery and her sitting in a wooden rocking chair. She smiled at the thought of such a perfect life. She was pulled back to the present with the sound of her students yelling her name.

Harold yelled and pointed, "Mrs. Jefferson, Lesley is walking down the road over there."

Hannah's heart skipped a beat. She asked the other teacher who had just come out to keep an eye on her kids, then she ran over to the area where Harold was pointing. Lesley must have squeezed between the opening of the fence over behind the trees. Hannah panicked even more. By the time she reached the road, Lesley was nowhere in sight.

Oh, my God. Where is that child? Why would she walk away? She knows better than that. What am I going to do? Lord, please help me find Lesley, Hannah prayed.

She headed back toward where her students were playing and lined them all up. Hannah's heart raced as she continued to look around. Mrs. Ramsey, another one of the third-grade teachers, was asking about what had happened. Hannah attempted to explain, but she felt she was having a panic attack. Amani walked up to her to return the radio Hannah had forgotten she'd handed to her. Mrs. Ramsey tried to get her to relax while she called the office on the walkie-talkie.

"Yes, we have a missing student," Mrs. Ramsey said. Hannah was trying to swipe her badge to let her students inside when she heard the assistant principal's response.

"Do you mean Lesley from Mrs. Jefferson's class?"

"Is that the student?" Mrs. Ramsey asked.

"Yes," Hannah said softly. Her heart pounded in her chest.

"Lesley is here in the office. Is Mrs. Jefferson out there?'

"Yes," Mrs. Ramsey replied.

Hannah knew she would be reprimanded and written up for this incident.

"Please tell her we'll have someone to watch her class so she can come up to my office."

"Will do."

Hannah felt as if she had two-hundred-pound weights on her legs. She led her students in as she trailed behind them. She saw them watching her. They looked afraid.

"Are you okay, Mrs. Jefferson?" Harold asked.

"Yes."

"Did they find Lesley?" questioned Amani.

"Yes," Hannah said, grateful they were steps away from the classroom now. She sped up in front of the class to unlock the door. As she let them in, Mrs. Riley, one of the kindergarten paraprofessionals was coming up the hall. Hannah turned on the lights and began to give her students instructions. She informed them to get out their AR book and work on the things they hadn't completed. Hannah thanked Mrs. Riley for watching her students and headed up to the office.

Walking in slow motion, she said several more prayers going up the hallway, feeling guilty for not talking to God for several days and for turning to alcohol instead of prayer. She reached the office door and took a deep breath. Hannah waited for the secretary to buzz her in. Her nerves on edge, Hannah took her time going to the back to Mrs. Watson's office. She stood for a moment, then knocked on the door.

"Come on in," Mrs. Watson said.

Hannah opened the door and felt relieved at the sight of Lesley working on a math worksheet at Mrs. Watson's table. *Thank goodness she's okay.*

"How are you, Mrs. Watson?" Hannah said, not knowing what else to say.

"I'm doing well. Come on and have a seat over here," she instructed, pointing to the chair in front of her desk. She then asked Lesley to go up front and finish working at the small table in the corner. "Don't go anywhere else. Do you understand?"

"Yes," Lesley said.

"Mrs. Jefferson, I know you've been through a lot."

"Yes, I have."

"I really hated to hear about your miscarriage."

"Thank you," Hannah said. She hadn't told them about the endometriosis and didn't plan to.

"Now, Mrs. Jefferson, please tell me how Leslie ended up on the street without you knowing?"

"To be honest, Mrs. Watson, I was feeling a little down, and I guess I was daydreaming. Then, Harold called out to me. I immediately ran over to get Lesley, but I didn't see her."

"That's because a parent happened to be coming by at that moment and saw Leslie leave the playground. She put her in the car and brought her up to the office. That parent was extremely upset. She wanted to know why there wasn't more supervision on our playground. I assured her that our teachers should be close to where the students are playing. Do you realize how many legal issues we would've been facing?"

"I'm so sorry, Mrs. Watson," Hannah said. "This will never happen again. I guess she moved so fast."

"These things can happen in seconds. That's why we have to stay close to the students and keep our eyes on them at all times. Thankfully, that parent promised to not say anything."

"Again, I apologize. I feel horrible."

"Mrs. Jefferson, I think you're a great teacher, and I know you love your students, but I'm going to have to write this up. I had to call Leslie's mom to inform her of what happened, and she was not happy. She stated you gave her an attitude when she met with you a few weeks ago. She's requesting Lesley be moved to another class."

"I didn't have an attitude. I only asked her to keep the conversation about Lesley."

"What did she say?"

"She asked if I had any children. I had just lost the baby," Hannah said, holding back tears.

"Mrs. Jefferson, we have to take time to grieve. When we try to throw ourselves back into our work, it's never a good thing."

"I'm learning that now."

"I'm also going to have to send you home without pay for two weeks. This could've turned out a whole different way," Mrs. Watson stated.

"I know, and I'm so sorry. I love my students. I don't want anything to happen to any of them. It's so hard. I feel like I'm never going to get the opportunity to be a mother. I don't know what I would have done if something would have happened to Lesley," Hannah sniffled, grabbing a tissue from the container on Mrs. Watson's desk.

"Let's just be grateful that we don't have to have that conversation. Hopefully, things will end with moving Lesley and your two weeks at home."

"I hope so too. I hate that. I enjoy teaching Lesley."

"I know you do. Please take some time to really get passed what you've experienced. We need you at one hundred percent."

"I will," Hannah said, standing to leave. She didn't know what else to do. She felt defeated. At the moment, all she could think about was getting to the women's Bible study tonight. She was tired—tired of the pain. Tired of the disappointment. Tired of trying to do things her way. Hannah wanted peace. She wanted to know the love she had heard so much about.

***

Later that evening, Hannah entered the doors of Giver of Life Ministries. Earlier, she had called Levi to tell him about her suspension. He could hardly make out what she was saying. She had cried until she felt there were no tears left. Levi had made it home about an hour later. They sat, ate dinner and talked more. Hannah then prepared for the women's Bible study group. She felt she had to get there. That's where her heart was leading her. She stood in the back for a moment listening to the worship team on stage. The lead was singing a verse that caught Hannah's attention. She looked up at the screen, noticing the title, "He Knows My Name." Hannah was soothed by the lyrics. She scanned the room for Ms. Priscilla and Robin. Everyone was on their feet, some with hands lifted, some in tears. She spotted them both next to each other with their hands also lifted and swaying to the song. Hannah headed over to the left side of the sanctuary. She slid in on the end next to Robin. Her friend smiled then started silently cheering as Hannah took her seat.

Hannah felt uncomfortable standing, so she listened and swayed to the song in her seat. The lyrics seemed to be written just for her. Hannah felt a tug at her heart. She knew this was where she needed to be. After the song ended, many across the sanctuary continued to sing the vamp to the song over and over. Hannah joined them. Before she knew what was happening, she was weeping, but this time, she felt more weights lifting off her shoulders. She kneeled beside Robin and begin to pray. Robin sat and rubbed her back, handing her a box of Kleenex.

He alone is my refuge, my place of safety... Hannah was comforted by God's words.

"Thank you, Lord, for loving me. Forgive me for choosing everything else but you. I pray for you to heal my heart. I bring my broken pieces to you. Please take me by the hand. Give me a miracle in my body. Help me to place all of my trust in you, Lord."

"Give it to him," Robin whispered as Hannah continued to cry. She remained on her knees. She wanted to stay right there. God's peace engulfed her. Hannah hadn't felt anything like it before. As she heard the sanctuary settle, Hannah climbed back onto her seat and tried to focus on the minister as she gave instructions about their breakout sessions. She remembered Ms. P telling her about the different rooms they broke up in. She liked the sound of a smaller group of people and women only. Yes, she could get with that. Unable to shake the scripture she had just heard, Hannah grabbed her phone and googled the words. Locating Psalm 91:2, Hannah went to the beginning and began reading the whole chapter.

After the minister finished giving the final instructions, everyone stood to head to their respective places. Hannah followed Robin into the room downstairs. Hannah sat all the way in the back, hoping they didn't have to speak or answer any questions. No such luck. Ms. P was already upfront introducing herself for any newcomers. She was the leader of the women's ministry and facilitator of the group. She informed them they would be talking and interacting for the next eight to twelve weeks.

"Our series is called We Thirst for You," Ms. Priscilla announced, locking eyes with Hannah. "In this study, we're going to study the story of Hannah and other women in scripture who were barren or desired something but later found out that God was the answer, but we won't stop there. We'll also study the meaning of the term *barren* and other places it's used in scripture and discover why. I'm excited to be here and even more excited to have you ladies here. We're going to get free together. Amen," Ms. Priscilla said, clapping.

"Amen," the other women in the room replied.

"Now, we're going to get started with a little opening activity. After that, we'll have a little fun. Before you leave, you'll be connected with someone, let's say an accountability partner. When you feel down and out or even giving up, you can call them or me. They'll pray with you and hold your confidence."

Hannah was nervous about the connection part. She was already connected. She whispered a prayer, asking God to deliver and help her to trust the others he would connect her with. She had to get to know them to share anything private with them. After the ice breaker, Ms. Priscilla begin calling the ladies up to the front to introduce themselves and explain what they wanted God to heal in their lives.

Hannah didn't feel comfortable sharing. She didn't know these women. She did want to be healed, but she wasn't ready to tell everyone. Her heart raced. She then began to relax a bit as she listened to the first woman and then another. She was amazed by their stories. Why was abuse so common? Hannah teared up as she listened to a woman about her mom's age speak. After she was done, Ms. P asked Hannah to go next.

CHAPTER NINETEEN

Saturday, June 15

Hannah sat on the floor in her home office organizing one of her new journals she had picked up from TJ Maxx. She had learned a method called bullet journaling. Pinterest had several ideas for using them to study the Bible. She had already created a table of contents, a section for prayer request, and made an area where she could list the scriptures she studied. Hannah was enjoying this time alone. She had pinned so many ideas. The instructions said she could use bulleted or a lined journals. Hannah had chosen both styles but decided to start with the bulleted one. She was enjoying how it was coming together. It was much like the graph paper she used in her math classes.

Hannah would be headed to her mother-in-law's in a few hours. Mama Jefferson had planned a late brunch at noon. Levi had gone ahead early to mow the lawn and assist her with a few things around the house. Hannah smiled, thinking about how proud his dad would be of him and how blessed he was to have such a great relationship with his mother. Months ago, Hannah wouldn't have been able to smile at such a thought, but today was a new day. A new journey. Her heart was open, and God was healing it one layer at a time.

So much had taken place in so little time, but she was much better, thanks to Christ. She had given her life over to him, and she felt like a new person. Hannah felt like David, one of her favorite people she'd read about in the Bible, when he slew the giant. She felt that God was helping her to slay several giants, including her lack of trust, which was melting away as she remained in his presence and continued to devour the scriptures. David was one of the most encouraging to read about. He poured out his heart to God after so much he'd done, and God delivered him, chose him and walked with him.

Over a month had passed since Hannah had heard from Brittany. She had texted and attempted to call Brittany numerous times with no response. Hannah replayed her hateful words to her sister, still regretting them. Her words caused her to miss the birth of her niece. Yes, her niece. It had taken Hannah sometime to call the baby her niece instead of her daughter. She didn't blame her sister for being angry with her. Hannah just hoped she wasn't alone while giving birth. She wished she could take it all back, but the damage was done. She really did miss Brittany.

God had begun to heal her heart in that area. He had also been dealing with Hannah's unforgiveness toward her mother. God had instructed her to continue to pray for her mom and sister each day, and she had.

Levi had forgiven Hannah for the statements she had made the night she was drunk. She had also forgiven him for walking out on her. He had told her he knew the words she spoke came from her pain. Levi promised to give her time to walk through her healing, and he had. Hannah knew many young women didn't have the same blessing of a husband, so she'd began to thank God daily for Levi's heart for her. They both had talked more about their feelings and vowed to trust each other more and to remember the wedding vows they'd made before God.

Hannah had added an oversized chair in the office for her prayer and devotional time and had kept the peach color after taking down the nursery, adding accessories to match it. It had really grown on her. Although she continued with the Progestin-only treatment, she was believing God for a miracle. Dr. Calhoun had requested that she remain on it for about six months. No matter how long the treatment lasted, Hannah prayed that she would keep her trust in God and not look at her situation.

Time alone with God was like a gift she had denied for years. She regretted it but had to look ahead and not behind. She could hear him speaking to her even more now. Being able to talk to him and ask him questions was something she always wanted. For the past few weeks, she had sat in his presence for hours at a time, listening and devouring the Word.

Hannah continued to attend the women's Bible study group each week since the night of her surrender. The women in the group felt like the family members she never had. She couldn't wait until next week. Surrendering to God was a refreshing feeling. Grabbing a pillow from the chair, Hannah kneeled and began to pray.

"Dear Lord, I come to you as humble as I know how, thanking you for another day. I thank you for covering Levi and me and our family. Father, I don't want to ask why anymore. I want to continue to draw closer to you. Forgive me for sinning against you. Forgive me for running away from you to people and what I thought would bring me happiness. Please continue to walk with me. Never leave me alone," Hannah cried. "Also, Father, can you help Brittany? She needs you. The baby needs you. Please continue to protect them. Help Brittany and Malik to obey you too. Help Brittany finish school and provide for the baby. Levi and I will do our best to help her where we can. Lord, save Mama, Aunt Loretta, and Malcolm. Help them to know you and be delivered. I pray for Mama to give you her pain as well. I could see it that day at her house. I know how she treated me, but I believe it's because of an even deeper hurt she has, not just about her losing Terrance. Please help all of us understand our true purpose. I want to live my life for you. In Jesus' name. Amen."

After her prayer, Hannah opened her Bible and sat it on the chair while she went to grab a cup of coffee. She also used her phone to search for lists of themed scriptures, but she loved flipping through the Bible to find them. When Hannah returned, she placed her coffee on the computer desk, placed the Bible on her lap and began reading. As she looked down, one of the scriptures that had previously brought tears to her eyes, jumped off the page at her.

Matthew 6:33, "But seek first His kingdom and His righteousness, and all these things will be added to you."

Hannah couldn't believe her eyes. The message was clear. God wanted her first as Ms. P and Mama Jefferson had shared. She needed to keep seeking him for herself. The waterworks began again. She felt God's love and peace all around her.

Give it all to me. I will heal you and make you whole again.

She answered, "Make me whole, Lord. I trust you." For the next hour, she devoured the scriptures. After reading several chapters of Matthew and stopping to journal, her heart was so full, she decided to call Ms. P.

'Hannah got up and went into the bedroom to grab her phone from the nightstand. School was out for the summer and Hannah was enjoying every second of it. It was 10:12, so Hannah knew Ms. P hadn't made it to the salon. She had told her she would be going in late on Saturdays during the summer. The phone rang twice before she answered.

"Hey, Ms. P.," Hannah stated, heading back into the office, taking a seat on the floor.

"Hey, sweetness. How are you?"

"I'm doing great."

"That's good to hear. I have been enjoying seeing you at the women's Bible study."

"I am loving it. I admit, I struggled a lot, but that night at your church was the moment I let down my guard and God moved through the crack."

"Amen. That's all he needs. He created us. Along the way, we stray from him. We sin against him, but he begins to draw us back, sometimes through our circumstances."

"I understand that more now than before."

"You see, there's nothing wrong with wanting a child or anything else. The problem comes when we make those things bigger than God—when we desire those things more, when those things have our hearts."

"I never realized I wanted something more than God."

"Sometimes we won't realize it. God or one of his servants has to reveal it to us. That's part of the cleansing process. God is changing your heart to love like him. He wants to use you."

"What do you mean?"

"As I've told you before, he's going to bring you out on the other side of this. He wants you to help other women, maybe even girls, to come out of their barren places as you are. Barren is physical and spiritual. We are body, soul and spirit. He wants to heal our whole self."

"Thanks for standing with me, Ms. P. I'm grateful and looking forward to growing in Christ."

"I'm looking forward to that as well. And if you allow me to, I will be here to walk with you."

"I would love that."

***

Hannah arrived at Mama Jefferson's an hour and a half later. She pulled next to their other car and got out. Hannah loved the four-bedroom single-family home sitting on a large corner lot. She admired the freshly planted flowers as she made her way to the door. Mama Jefferson had a green thumb.

She kept it looking beautiful. Hannah rang the doorbell a few times before Levi answered.

"Hey, babe," Levi said, leaning in to kiss her.

Hannah kissed him tenderly before saying, "Hello, husband. Did you finish up the yard for Mama Jefferson?"

"Yes, and I'm finishing changing out that chandelier in the dining room. Come on in. Mama's in the kitchen finishing up."

"It smells good up in here."

"Yes. I can't wait to wrap my lips around her homemade biscuits," Levi said, pretending to lick his fingers.

"You are so greedy," Hannah said as they shared a laugh before she followed him into the large eat-in kitchen. Mama Jefferson was spreading butter over her homemade biscuits. Hannah's mouth watered.

"Hey, Mama," Hannah announced.

Mama Jefferson placed the pan on the counter, wiped her hands on her apron and gave Hannah a big hug.

"It's good to see you, baby. Go get washed up. I'm just about done. We can sit, eat and talk in a little bit."

"Okay," Hannah said, turning around and going into the downstairs bathroom. Levi disappeared into the dining room.

Seconds later Mama Jefferson called them back into the kitchen. Hannah entered first, her eyes wide.

Did Mama Jefferson think she was cooking for an army?

"This is a lot of food," Hannah stated. "Are you taking some of it over to the church?"

"Oh, yes. Gotta keep feeding God's people," Mama Jefferson said, waving Hannah over to sit. She set down a pan of sausage and took a seat. Hannah sat next to Mama Jefferson. She used Hannah to sample the different items. Hannah thought everything was delicious as usual. Levi came in a few minutes later and sat across from them.

"Mama, are you still going by to see Ms. Agnes at the nursing home today?" Levi asked.

"I plan to."

"Tell her I said hello when you see her. I hope she's feeling better."

"I will. She is getting there. Thank you for joining me this morning," Mama Jefferson said, looking at Hannah.

"Thank you for inviting me."

"Well, I've had a talk with knucklehead right here."

"Really, Mama?" Levi replied.

"Yes. I wanted to talk to you two together," Mama Jefferson continued, handing Levi and Hannah a plate. She then bowed her head and begin to pray. "Heavenly Father, we come to you as humble as we know how thanking you for being on this side, first of all, and thanking you for the opportunity to get it right with you. Father, you are a good, good father. I pray my son and daughter-in-love will continue to walk with you. I pray you strengthen Hannah in this process that she must walk through to come out on the other side. In Jesus' name I pray. Amen."

"Amen," Hannah and Levi repeated. Hannah was grateful for the prayer.

"Alright, let's dig into this good food," Levi said, rubbing his hands together.

Hannah dropped some grits, eggs, a few pieces of sausage and a biscuit on her plate. She couldn't resist Mama Jefferson's cooking.

"So, how are you feeling?" Mama Jefferson asked as Hannah picked up her fork.

"I'm doing better."

"That's good. I know the treatments you're taking are frustrating."

"They are," Hannah replied.

"I'm praying against any serious side effects. God's got you."

"I know. And thank you for all of the prayers and encouragement."

"You're welcome."

Levi remained silent.

"Know that you are a blessing. You are loved and accepted. I wish I could sit down and talk to your mama and help her through whatever deeply rooted issues she's experienced because she has to have gone through something to be so mean to her own children."

"I think she has," Hannah said, digging into her grits and eggs.

"One of the things I've never agreed with is how our community sweeps so much under the rug. People raise their children up talking about, 'What happens in my house stays in my house' and all this other mess. We have to get free. I see so many broken young ladies over at the church. I'm so tired of hearing the same stories of how mama and daddy treated them awful. God can't be pleased with many of us. Then we holler, 'Do what I say, not what I do.' I could go on and on, but I want you to heal completely, you hear me."

"Yes, ma'am," Hannah responded, finishing her grits.

"You are an amazing young lady—intelligent, got your head on straight, and not to mention you put up with my big-head son."

Levi gave Mama Jefferson the side eye. Hannah burst out laughing.

"Thank you," Hannah said.

"Just remember, honey, your mama is broken. I was broken at one point in my life. Sometimes people don't always know that they're broken. They have to come to God and allow him to show them. They also have to allow him to heal them, or they'll remain broken. Jesus died for our brokenness. You hear me?"

"Yes, ma'am," Hannah replied, nibbling on her biscuit.

"And you know what else?"

"What?" Hannah asked.

"You, my love, are broken." Hannah nodded in agreement.

"And I'm glad I finally opened up and began to give it all to God."

"Thank you, Lord. He will do it. I saw your pain when I met you years ago, but you covered it well. It just rose up more when you lost the baby and got that diagnosis, then even more when your sister changed her mind about the adoption. When you called me that night weeping and your words slurring, my heart broke for you, and I knew I needed to intercede. As Levi was growing up, his dad and I taught him that married couples will sometimes have to walk through some things, and you must walk through them together. Then, he showed up over here and almost got knocked out for leaving you at home. That's when I knew I needed to intercede even more. I love you like my own, Hannah. Know that I am here for you. Don't hesitate to call me when you need me. This walk with Christ isn't always easy, but it is well worth it."

"Thank you."

"God loves you and your sister. He won't disappoint you. Your sister will come around, and your mama will too. You just keep praying for them."

"Thank you for sharing truth with me. I'll keep moving forward, allowing God to heal me."

"He will, everywhere you hurt."

After hanging out with Mama Jefferson for another hour, Levi followed Hannah home to drop off her car. They decided to hang out a bit, walk around the mall, maybe even head over to the Tanger Oulet. They didn't want to waste this beautiful day. Hannah wanted them to do this more often. Since they had married, they hardly got out. They only went from work to home most of the time. They were still young. They could work and purposely schedule dates. Maybe they could even plan a staycation one of these weekends and head over to one of those nice hotels in downtown Buckhead. *That would be nice,* Hannah thought. Most of all, she wanted them to focus on making good memories as they continued to trust in God for an addition to their family.

EPILOGUE

Monday, September 7

A new school year had gotten under way, and Hannah was glad for this three-day holiday weekend. It was Labor Day, and Hannah decided to celebrate Levi's twenty-seventh birthday today. Their house was filled with laughter as their family chatted and moved about. Hannah had sent a text to Brittany on yesterday, inviting her to join them. She prayed her sister would come. Hannah was thankful that her dad, aunt and uncle were off. Mama Jefferson was retired, so all she had to do was let her know what time to be there. Levi's official birthday would be this coming Thursday. She had planned a small getaway for the following weekend.

Mama Jefferson had come into the dining room and begun sharing baby stories with Hannah and her dad. Levi was begging her to stop embarrassing him. Hannah had heard the same stories hundreds of times but loved to hear them, so she could visualize what their kids would possibly be like. Because of the things she'd endured when she was small, she could hardly recall any of her younger years, and her mom hadn't allowed her dad to see her back then. Her dad shared those rare memories he did have from her toddler years.

Mama Jefferson and Aunt Melissa were making a spread. Aunt Melissa was in the kitchen preparing the mac and cheese and potato salad. Mama Jefferson had already prepared the deviled eggs and collard greens, and Uncle Joseph was out back on the grill. Hannah stood to see how the meat was coming along.

Stepping out the sliding glass door, she called out to her uncle, "How's it going, Uncle Joseph?" She stood next to him. He was aging more, and Hannah wanted him to go ahead and retire. He was a workaholic, but it seemed to be wearing on him. He looked tired but insisted on cooking the meat so Levi could relax.

"Some of the burgers are done. That's about it."

"Okay. How long do you think it will need?"

"Probably another hour or so."

"Sounds good. I appreciate you doing this for Levi."

"You know how much I love to grill, and Levi is like a son."

"I remember when you didn't feel that way about him."

"Oh, now you wanna go there. I just had to check the dude out, make sure he was good people."

"Did you and Daddy have to interrogate him and threaten his life when I brought him over to meet you all?"

"He's still alive, right?"

"Thankfully," Hannah said, laughing.

"Hannah, you have a visitor," Aunt Melissa said from the patio door.

"Who is it, Auntie?"

"Come and see for yourself."

Hannah didn't know what her aunt was up to. She quickly turned, leaving the conversation between her and Uncle Joseph. When she got to the door, she froze at the sight. Her prayers had been answered. Hannah's hands flew over her mouth, and tears began to flow at the sight of Brittany and the baby. Her sister smiled at her and waved her inside. Mama Jefferson stood next to her with her hands held up as if she was praying. Hannah stepped inside and nearly ran to embrace her sister. Levi grabbed the baby as she and Brittany held each other and cried. As Hannah attempted to apologize again, Brittany stopped her.

"There's no need for another apology. You're my sister, and I love you. I was hurt by your treatment that day, but I had a long time to think about how it all made you feel."

"I missed you, Brit," Hannah said, pulling away and reaching for the baby. She took a seat on the couch and began rocking her niece's small frame in her arms.

"I missed you too," Brittany replied, sitting next to Hannah.

"So, what did you name her?"

"You and Levi named her, remember?"

"What do you mean?"

"When I heard you say Neveah, it just stuck with me. I named her Neveah Grace Hamilton."

"Oh, my goodness. That's beautiful. She's beautiful."

"Thank you," Brittany replied. "Say hello to Auntie Hannah." The baby cooed as if she were trying to respond. Hannah and Brittany laughed.

"Ah, look at that face. Hi, Auntie's little princess," Hannah kissed her on the cheek and held her closer. She was thankful for another chance—a chance to get to know such a precious little one. Although she wished she hadn't missed her birth, she believed that God had truly shown her grace today.

Everyone went back to what they had been doing. Mama Jefferson offered to take Neveah to allow Hannah and Brittany time to catch up. Hannah reluctantly handed Neveah to her mother-in-law. Smiling from ear to ear, Mama Jefferson headed into the dining room with the baby. Hannah knew she was ready to spoil her niece rotten.

"So how have you been?" Hannah asked.

"It's been okay. Being a mother is rewarding and difficult at the same time."

"I bet. So, did you have to move back in with Mama?"

"Girl, no. I did call and ask, and the answer was still no. My friend, Kelsey, allowed us to move in with her. She's been helping with Neveah as much as she can. I was also able to receive a discount on childcare for the days I have no help and have to work or study."

"That was nice of her to allow you to move in. And know that I'm here to help as well, as much as I can. I'm so glad you're here."

"So am I."

"So, what's up with Travis?"

"Girl, the same. He only cares about his career, so I didn't even call when she was born."

"Wow. I'll put him on my prayer list."

"Your prayer list?"

"Yes, sis. I gave my life to Christ, and I feel so at peace now."

"I knew there was something different."

"Yes, and I want you to come with me to this awesome women's Bible study group on Wednesdays. They have childcare there at the church."

"Cool. I would love to come."

Hannah smiled at her sister and thanked God again for all he had done in her. She also thanked him for Brittany and Neveah's safety and shelter. At that moment, she knew she had truly changed.

She felt no anger.

She felt no jealousy.

She felt no fear that motherhood wouldn't happen for her too.

She felt no rejection.

She only felt love and peace—the love and the peace of God as well as the love and peace that came from knowing he had sent so many blessings into her life.

***

That evening, after their family had gone home, Levi sat out on the patio talking to his friend, Quinton, who had arrived late from a family get-together at his mother-in-law's. His wife didn't come with him this time. Hannah guessed she should reach out to her more. Hannah was back in her office sitting at her desk with a blank piece of paper in front of her. After talking to Brittany, she was more worried about her mom. Brittany had told her she had been to see her and continued to call and check on her. Each time, Brittany said she'd had been drinking. Hannah had tried calling her, too, but her phone would go to voicemail, so she planned to write her in hopes that she would read it.

Hannah couldn't give up on her mom. She knew what God had done in her life, and she wanted the same for her mother. She sat for several more minutes, trying to figure out what to say. After a few more minutes, she bowed her head and prayed for God to lead her. Then, she began writing:

Dear Mama,

I don't know where to begin. I guess I'll just start. I'm writing you to tell you I forgive you. You're probably saying, "I don't need you to forgive me," but Mama, you broke my heart. It was hard living at Aunt Loretta's and feeling like I couldn't talk to anyone but my one friend back then. I longed for you to come and see me, but you only called when you found out that Daddy was coming to see me, after you kept me from him for so long.

I forgive you for not being a part of my life. I forgive you for not believing me when I told you about my molestation. I forgive you for choosing others over me. I forgive you for your many words that broke my spirit. I forgive you for making me feel like a burden instead of a blessing. I forgive you, and I love you. I know that you drink because there is some hidden pain that goes deeper than losing your first husband. Mama, something or somebody broke you. Because of that, you mistreated me, even more than Malik and Brittany. I now know that

168

I should have been depending on God's love and not anyone else's. I struggled to trust him for many years, but now I've given my life over to him and pray that someday you will too.

There is so much I've wanted to tell you. It was so hard to see my classmates and friends with their moms. I had to get passed you not being at my high school graduation, my college graduation and then my wedding. It wasn't easy, and I never stopped hoping that you would come around.

I know you don't care for Daddy and this side of my family, but they have been amazing in my life. I hope you will someday come to some of our get-togethers and meet them. I'll never stop loving you, and I will continue praying for your healing from the inside out.

Love Always,
Your Daughter,
Hannah

RESOURCES

The references to endometriosis and its treatments were taken from various sources. To learn more about the condition and become more educated on some of the dangerous side effects, visit the sites below.

www.hopkinsmedicine.org

www.brighamandwomens.org

www.panadiahealth.com

www.mayoclinic.org

www.summitmedicalgroup.com

NOTE FROM THE AUTHOR

I hope you enjoyed reading Barren Womb. Although the majority of the story is fictional, the core of it relates to me (the physical and spiritual barrenness). This book is near and dear to my heart because God walked with me through my physical battle with endometriosis. Through the many procedures and attempted treatments, I could not have made it without my Lord and Savior, Jesus Christ.

In addition to the physical aspect of barrenness, the LORD also brought me out of my spiritual barren places. I have walked through depression and many disappointments. I, like Hannah, believed that other things and people would fill my empty places. I pray that you would also surrender to God whatever has caused barrenness in your life. As you learned from Hannah's story, our physical barrenness can bring forth the spiritual barrenness that was already in us. Be free in Christ.

Join the "No Longer Barren" campaign. It is more than a slogan. I pray that you will simply declare that you will allow God to heal you totally and completely and never again depend on other people or things to do what only God can.

You might be asking, "Is that it?"

Yes, it is. However, it is not as easy as it seems. You see, you have to release all of your burdens to Christ, everything that is keeping you from being free in Him. I learned the hard way that my emptiness could never be filled by things, desires and People because it was where God wanted to dwell.

-Author Denise M. Walker

ABOUT THE AUTHOR

As many others, Denise M. Walker has walked through many obstacles, struggling to overcome depression, rejection and fear from youth to adulthood. Today, with Christ, Denise can be described as nothing less than an overcomer.

Denise M. Walker is a minister, wife, mother, podcaster, experienced educator and entrepreneur. Denise has educated youth for over 20 years and has served in the field of education for 23 years. Most of her career, she has taught at the middle school level and mentored preteen and teen girls.

Denise is the founder of Hope-in-Christ Ministries, Inc. and the owner of Armor of Hope Writing & Publishing Services, LLC. In addition, she is the creator and facilitator of the Hope-in-Christ Book Club Facebook group, the host of Hope-in-Christ w/Denise and Building Literacy & True Identity podcasts. She is also a co-host of the Release Her Sound Radio Show.

Her ministry's mission is to lead others to the truth of Christ, build literacy, and assist individuals in walking in their true identity in Him.

Websites: www.hope-in-christ.com (Ministry).
www.armorofhopewritingservices.com (Business) and
www.denisemwalker.com (Author)

Denise can also be followed on various social media sites:
Twitter: @author_denise, @Hope_in_Christ1
Facebook Fan Pages: @AuthorDeniseMWalker,
@projecthope.mytrueidentity, @HopeInChristMinistriesInc
Book Club: Hope-in-Christ Book Club
Instagram: @authordenisemwalker, @my_true_identity_h.o.p.e._
@hope_in_christ1, @hopeinchristbookclub
 LinkedIn: Author Denise M Walker

Her emails are denise@hope-in-christ.com, info@denisemwalker.com

Amazon Author page: amazon.com/author/denisew

OTHER BOOKS BY THIS AUTHOR

1. Hannah's Hope - Book 1 (My True Identity Teen Series)

2. Hannah's Heart – Book 2 (My True Identity Teen Series)

3. Re-Presenting God: Taking a Healthy Look at the Holy One of Israel (Youth Bible journal)

4. Is This English Class or Bible Study? (Bible Strategies)

5. The S.C.R.I.P.T. (Beginners journal for aspiring Christian authors)

STAY TUNED....

Book 2 of The Redemption Series – *An Unlikely Miracle*

Book 3 of the My True Identity Series – *Purposed & Loved*

Book 2 – *Is This English Class or Bible Study? Strategies for Building Literacy and Studying God's Word*

BE KIND, LEAVE A REVIEW

If you enjoyed Hannah's story, please leave a review on Amazon, Good Reads, Barnes & Noble, Apple Books and/or SCRIBD.

Thank you! God's blessings to you!

Made in the USA
Columbia, SC
01 October 2020

21681915R00098